I0731504

1814

BY THE DAWN'S EARLY LIGHT

By *Tecla Emerson*

1814 By the Dawn's Early Light
© 2022 by Tecla Emerson

ISBN: 978-1-7377615-4-9

Printed in the United States of America
Published by OutLook Press
Pub3000@aol.com

Edited by Colonel Richard C. Murphy, USMC, Retired

Cover design by
K. Sodergreen
Sodergreen@aol.com

Interior layout by
Robert Louis Henry
RightHandPublishing.com

Dedicated to
Ensign Alex Rott and Cadet Katharine E. Rott
...so proudly we hail

"Then, in that hour of deliverance, my heart spoke. Does not such a country, and such defenders of their country, deserve a song?"

—Francis Scott Key (1814)

EARLY LIGHT...

Debris hung in scraggly twists from aged branches. Branches bent and broken from past storms. It had been more than a few days since the big blow. How it had crept up on us so fast was anyone's guess.

'Course the watermen saw it coming and had high-tailed it to shore. That is 'cept Matthew, but that was not unusual for him, being the youngest of the watermen and all. He had his sails up so that meant he was done for the day. He ran before the wind. That's how he described it. Well, and I might add he just made it! But then that was Matthew – forever the risk-taker.

Now, the breeze came in light puffs. It was just enough to move the bits of dangling seagrasses that hung from the trees. It was a sight to see, I'll say that, and maybe one I'd never see again. Well, that was my hope.

It had been a most terrible storm and it was

a wonder that any of it had been cleaned up. It had been on a sweltering day - I remember that much. There had been an odd color to the sky, maybe something like the color of pea soup. The soup I tried to avoid whenever possible, should anyone care. But that storm had been rumbling and moving in from the west. There had been dark angry, roiling clouds that had piled on top of each other. For a while, they seemed to stop. That was when I was sure I saw a long squiggly line snaking its way down from the southern edge. A tornado it was called - but it was hard to make out at that distance. It was so far away.

But then the drenching, pounding rain and wind. I'd never seen the like. It pounded our little island. It seemed like it would last forever, but I was quite sure it hadn't gone on for more than a few minutes before continuing on its way.

Now, just these many days later, there were still signs of the havoc it had caused. We were fortunate having lost only a few shingles from the barn and a few torn from the roof of the house. 'Course the way our house was built, angled to the west and all, the brunt of the storm was lessened. Pa said we'd get cooler breezes in the summer with the house set that way. He built it, so I guess he knew what he was about.

Two of our sheep were still missing but maybe one day they'd turn up. It was doubtful though. The Brits had been helping themselves to just about anything that could be eaten, and they'd been on a raid at the other end of the island more than once, taking anything they could get their hands on.

But with that storm! Our cow had thankfully been safely tucked back in the barn. We had a habit of trying to keep her out of sight. The chickens, of course, knew to run for cover.

Storm or not, we were most often cautious as those Brits were giving us fits. Who knew what they'd be up to next? Thankfully, we were tucked away up at the far end of the island, away from where they were anchored. They'd raided our island before, so we knew to stay to ourselves.

And now, with everyone gone, I'd been left with the work of bringing in what was left of the corn. Not my favorite chore to be sure! And that storm had knocked over more than a few of the stalks, which of course made it even more difficult to harvest. But Pa had said leave them as they were, in their awkward positions and they'd more'n likely still be good, regardless.

And, he added, almost in a whisper, if we don't harvest them, the Brits certainly will. What he didn't say was that we needed that corn to get us through the winter!

Where to start? There wasn't all that much left, but Pa had said I was to go down the rows and salvage all that could be used. Some we could keep for us to eat, and much of the rest could be easily stored for the winter months for the animals.

I was alone. Pa had gone to the mainland. He said he wanted to check on Mum. But he'd also had the tobacco to deliver. It was ready and he had to get it to the mainland. Course I was quite sure it had more to do with his concern of more bad weather approaching, or that those Brits would be out this way and help themselves to what was left.

He hadn't been a tobacco farmer before. Pa that is. Like everything else, he just learned by doing. He said his family had been fur trappers over in Delaware. That was before he ran away and found work on one of those merchant ships.

He knew well enough of the dangers of being on a sailing ship what with the Brits scouring the coast. They'd captured many an American vessel as well as many unsuspecting boys and men. And sure enough, they got him. He didn't talk about it much but now one of his biggest concerns was in being recaptured.

He knew it was best to stay out of sight. He actually had a disguise that he was sure would get past any that wanted to stop him. If truth be known, it was truly kinda funny, and we had a good laugh over it more than once. He dressed as a very old, stooped-over farmer. We giggled every time he got up into that garb: ripped pants, a ratty hat, no shoes and he'd walk with a cane all bent over. Even worse, when anyone talked to him, he'd go "Aaahhhh?" as though he were stone deaf. It really made us laugh to the point we had to hold our sides. My pesky twin brothers would beg him to do it again and again even when he didn't have to travel off the farm.

There was danger if they discovered him. The disguise would, with luck, keep him out of the hands of the Brits so it was not to be toyed with. He was careful but kept everything handy should there be a need. If he was recognized things would not go well for him.

Some days I wished they'd discover me and carry me off to some grand adventure. I knew that wasn't a good thought. There had to be other ways of getting off this lonely and lost piece of desolate land, but I hadn't come up with one yet.

Thankfully our farm was very small, hardly worth the trip if those Brits thought to restock with more supplies. It was also a ways from where they'd dropped anchor, so chances were we were safe from any invasion.

We had enough to feed ourselves and usually some left over to sell. Pa felt it was a fine and comfortable life and we shouldn't be lusting over too much more. We all had our freedom, what more could we want? He may have been thinking of that Revolutionary War and how we were now safe from English rule – but that was a while ago, 1775 to be exact – long before I was born.

Course no one ever asked me how I felt about living on a farm and so far from everything. My thought was, should they care, I could have used a little more adventure or excitement in my life. Seemed like all I did was work from dawn 'til dusk. If I wasn't in the field helping Pa, I'd be making candles or churning butter or salting down the fish with Mum. There was no end to it. Chores in the morning, chores at night. Rarely did I find any time for anything that I wanted to do.

But Pa loved where we were. He said it was uncommonly peaceful.

He was considerably older than Mum and after all those years of being in captivity as an impressed seaman with the British Navy, he was grateful to be alive and to be comfortably situated on this remote island somewhere in the Chesapeake Bay. He felt that we were all fortunate to be able to enjoy a good life and that we were safe, tucked away on this far away spit of land. Well safe anyway until those Brits decided to anchor offshore and help themselves to anything they found.

Earlier Pa had told me that he'd be heading to the mainland. "Mackenzie," he'd said, "I've loaded the tobacco. And will check on Mum and the boys. And" he added, "If luck and the tides are with me, I'll be back by nightfall." And that's what he'd said.

Well, I was quite sure something must be up as he rarely addressed me by my full name. And he certainly was concerned about those boys! So off he went! He knew he was taking a chance with the Brits so close by. If they recognized him, they'd surely grab him again. He did have his old man outfit packed in his bag should it be needed.

"I just don't understand it," I said.

Yes, I had started talking to myself. It made me feel not quite so alone. With everyone gone, including two of the peskiest younger brothers to ever have been put on the face of the earth - well with all of them off to the mainland it was truly lonely.

The basket was nearly filled with the ears of corn. "Dang," I said as I tried to lift it. If I tucked anymore in, I wouldn't be able to heft it back to the barn. Pa had Gertie, our only horse, so there was no choice. Lifting the basket, the two handles groaned from the weight. I had other words that wanted to come out, but they didn't.

My feet knew the way as they carried me down the path. The basket got heavier with each step. I lowered it to the ground so's I could stop for a moment to catch my breath. The corner of my once clean apron, now soiled and wrinkled, was used to wipe the dripping sweat.

"Now," I said out loud, "What could that possibly be?" There were dots hovering out on the Bay. They were along the horizon, too far away to identify. It was even hard to tell which way they were heading. I didn't even want to think about more big ships off our shore. They hadn't passed this way earlier unless it was during the night so they must be heading up the Bay.

"Let's just hope they don't stop here," I said to no one. But then, there wasn't a soul around to hear me. I was alone.

Or so I thought.

LAND OF THE FREE . . .

And then there was Rip. Lord, he was bothersome.

"Macky, Wacky, what're you doin'?"

There is nothing on this earth peskier than an 11-year-old boy! He was worse, by far than my two brothers and they had just turned eight!

I knew he didn't really care what I was doing, and didn't he just love to make a mess of my name. It was Mackenzie but he had never used my proper name, usually shortening it to just Mac.

But there he was. Again!

I knew that all he wanted to do was gather more information so's he could tease me or go to town and tease someone else with anything that he learned. It was his favorite pastime – teasing the girls. I wondered if anyone even liked him.

He was four years younger than me. He was not only a tease but was rude, mannerless and of little value to anyone that I could see. My brothers would often get into mischief with him and thought he was funny, but they were the only ones. He was what was known as a freed black or anyhow that's what they called him. And maybe not quite "freed", as far as we knew, but no one had ever called him anything else. Slave trade had been outlawed just a few years ago, or anyways they weren't supposed to be bringing more into the country. But as Pa said, and he was one to know, he very much doubted that it had stopped. Slave transportation was still going on whether we cared or not.

But, as far as Rip was concerned Pa liked him well enough, although I can't imagine why! He did say that boy had more common sense than any other young one he'd ever met. But then Rip liked to help Pa and Pa certainly needed the extra hands especially when it came time for the harvest.

"What is it," I asked knowing the teasing would be nonstop if I didn't at least acknowledge that he was standing there.

"How come you not wit' your brothers?" he asked. It was perplexing how he always knew everyone's business.

"They're sick." I could have made something up, but it was easier to just answer the question,

I had work to do.

"How come they sick?" he asked. He pulled his hat with the tattered brim a bit lower making it impossible to see his eyes.

Well, he already knew 'cause he knew everything. But just answer him I thought, so's I could get back to work.

"Measles," I answered. That should keep him away from me! I hefted the basket up to my hip.

"Measles, weasles," he started to taunt.

Lord if he'd just go away. What can one say to a young orphan boy with no family? Rip was one who no one seemed to give much thought to. He was just there. Guess no one much cared really, 'cept me 'cause he was such an annoying pest. But then I regretted my bad thoughts. Yes, he was an orphan, 'course that didn't give him leave to be such a vexation all the time – at least to me.

"When they comin' back?"

"They'll be back soon enough," I said, trying to be dismissive and hoping he'd move on to pester whoever else was on this godforsaken island. Oh my I thought, I didn't mean to be so hateful. But I didn't say it aloud!

"Why'd ya cut yer hair?" he asked, his voice

a singsong whine.

"You know very well why," I answered. My breath was coming in short gasps, but I was almost to the barn.

"'Cause ya Mum told ya to," he mimicked. "Said wit' the sickness that was goin' round it would make yer life a whole bit easier." This was followed by a "Ha!" He wanted to be sure I knew that there was nothing he didn't already know about.

I was tired of listening to him – already! I was sorely tempted to lash out or at least throw an ear of corn at him. But I knew how that would end and decided to hold my temper. And he knew good and well if he'd been on the mainland near any of those plantations, he never would've gotten away with sassing a white person.

"Did you see those ships?" I asked as I lowered the basket. I wiped the sweat from my forehead. I was still going to have to spend time separating out the ears for the animals and for us.

"What you talkin' about?" he asked.

Ah, I had him. Something I knew that he didn't. "Why just south of here. They're there on the horizon."

This took him back down the path so's I could have a moment of peace. I tried to work quickly. The pile of corn for the animals was getting bigger, but there were a few ears left to bring into the house. Separating the ears wasn't so hard and the basket was much lighter when I made my way back down the path.

He was still there. Would he ever leave? "Well, lookie there," he said. "There's a bunch of them."

I opened the door into our kitchen and closed it with more force than necessary. He wouldn't dare follow me into the house, so I was safe from his endless chattering and teasing. I could hear him muttering and his infernal, endless, senseless whistling. He loved imitating a mourning dove with its low, sad call. He was good at it too, much as I hated to admit it. It was difficult to tell when it was his whistle or when it was the actual call of a dove. I would have liked to learn how to do it, but he said it wasn't for girls. Only boys could whistle. Well just wait I thought. One day I'll show him.

But he'd lost interest and was obviously leaving, as the whistling got fainter. No doubt he was thinking up some way to pester someone else.

"Phew," I said, but not too loud. The evening was mine. Pa had said he'd try to return to-night, but if his intention was to check on Mum and the two boys, and get the tobacco to market, I thought chances were slim that he'd be able to get back, what with the Brits questioning and detaining anyone they saw.

He knew what he was doing and with luck and his good sense, he'd dodge them all again. He'd done it a few times already and was more than pleased with his success with his odd disguise as an almost deaf, very old and bent-over farmer.

But here I was and staying alone wasn't my favorite thing. I'd done it once before and made it through without any trouble but had never been happy all by myself.

Checking the bar once more that held the door closed, I went to work with the corn while humming to myself. Humming a tune was my way of drowning out any of the outside noises that came through the dark. I was successful but still decided to turn in early. I could finish with the corn tomorrow.

HOME OF THE BRAVE…

The sun no doubt was peeking over the horizon. I opened my eyes with reluctance. I hadn't meant to sleep so long. I could have slept a whole lot longer, 'cept for the flock of geese that flew over. They certainly could make quite the racket. No doubt they wanted to let the world know they were moving on before the winter weather settled in.

The sun was just starting to welcome the day as I made my way to the barn. Dew was heavy on the grass soaking the hem of my skirt. Flossie was waiting for me, her huge dark eyes wanted to stare me down. She wanted me to know that I was late. But then, she didn't have too much milk left anyhow. Pa was either going to have to breed her fairly soon or find another milch cow. But that really wasn't for me to worry over. For now, I just needed to get her milked.

Easy enough as there wasn't all that much that she'd give anymore. The pail wasn't heavy as the warm, white liquid sloshed over the sides. The handle was loose and squeaked with each step.

And then there they were.

Did I really not see them on the way to the barn? There was an entire flotilla of ships – as Pa would call it. All looked to be at anchor. Their sails were tied securely to the yardarms. They were too far offshore to see well, but it looked like some sailors were busy on the decks, moving about as though each had some sort of mission.

I think I groaned. More than a few were already at anchor over near the other side of our Island. Why were more coming in? Of course, I knew. There was a war on. I did know that much. They were calling it the War of 1812, even though it was already 1814! But then Pa liked to call it the second war for independence! Independence from Britain! But I thought we already had that. Independence that is.

And there they were, anchored in our Bay! How could this be I wondered? But I'd been told more than once to be cautious. I was actually told by Mum to stay out of sight of any of the soldiers. If they came round, they'd be up to no good. She said hide in the cold cellar and don't dare come out 'til they were long gone. I also knew to keep our animals close.

The Brits were hungry. It seemed that their mission was to clear our little island of all the food that we produced, including our animals. Pa had cautioned more than once that we were at war with them, and they'd stop at nothing to win a victory.

Now, it looked like more were arriving. This I was sure wasn't good. Where was Pa? Would he be returning today? Did he risk being captured? Had he already been captured?

He had headed into St. Michael's on the mainland to get the tobacco sold and to check on Mum and the boys. He said it shouldn't take more than a day, two at most. But now, where was he?

Somehow this didn't seem fair, but with all the animals to care for, someone had to stay back. They'd decided that I'd be the one. There was no one else to tend to the farm. Mum's father wasn't that far away, him being the Poplar Island preacher and all, but he loathed Pa. Regardless, Mum said if I needed anything, go on over and ask. Chances were he wouldn't refuse me even though he had little to do with our family.

It was no secret. This was after all a very small island. But he would never accept that Mum had married an *off-islander* as he was often called.

Grandfather's family had lived on the Island since just after the last massacre. That was when the Indians wanted to reclaim their territory and had wiped out all of the islanders. That was probably almost 200 years ago. Terrible, but were they any worse than the Brits?

It wasn't all that long ago when they landed here and burned every house on the entire island. The Brits that is! It was during the Revolutionary War, which actually wasn't all that long ago. It was late in the 1700s but Mum's father, the preacher, had just started his own church when it happened. They burned that too. He still had ill feelings towards the Brits. Needless to say, we weren't their friends. I needed to stop thinking like this but now look what was happening?

There was nothing I could do. And I had my chores and regardless of all the other tasks ahead of me, Pa had said get the corn in should we have another blow, which would surely be the ruin of the little we had left. Well, most of it was in.

We had a trap door near the hearth. When lifted it revealed a cool storage room under the floor. That's where we usually kept most of our harvest: corn, beets, carrots, pumpkins, and whatever else Pa had planted. We kept the flour down there too, and cornmeal, which was always a problem. The mice liked it as much as we did. They didn't care that it was all tucked up in wooden barrels. It didn't prevent them from trying to chew their way through the slats.

But Mum had said that was where I was to go if the Brits decided to raid our farm. It was a great hiding place should they come calling. It was doubtful however that they'd ever get all the way out here as we were too far away from where most of the Islanders lived.

I covered the pail of milk and brought it down the ladder to the cellar where it would stay cool. I'd work with it later. Churning butter was not on my list of tasks for today. I had to get back out there. With one eye watching out the window, I pulled off my already dirty clothes and tossed my apron aside and changed into my favorite outfit: oversized breeches. Until recently they had been unused and tucked away in a chest, but then I'd found them. I pulled them out, along with the tattered linen shirt that had been Pa's. Mum had decided it was going to be cut up and pieced to go into the next quilt. After all, she had used nearly every scrap of used clothing we'd ever owned. The last that she'd made, was a gaily patterned one that kept me warm on most winter nights.

Maybe it wasn't important, but Pa had said - without Mum hearing - that I'd be better off looking like a young boy if those pillaging Brits saw me. He didn't want Mum to be overly concerned and I didn't question that at all, just figured maybe he was right. But best of all, I loved running free in the long pants instead of the skirt that always wanted to tangle around my legs and trip me. And if that wasn't enough, all those yards and yards of fabric could be dreadfully hot in the summer months.

When no one was around, or they were all busy with their tasks, and not paying me any heed, I'd tuck my billowing skirt up into my apron sash. That way it couldn't trip me, and it was lots cooler. Mum caught me once and she was so annoyed with my behavior.

"No lady would ever be caught in such disarray," she'd said. But then as she demanded that I return my skirt to its rightful decorum and turned to walk away, I thought I saw her smiling. In any case, I was more careful, and she hadn't caught me doing it again.

But this was much better. I pulled the rope tight that kept my britches from falling down. Pa's hat was a close enough fit. It would keep the sun from burning my scalp and turning me any darker.

Whenever Rip was in a particularly teasing mood, he would call me an Indian. I'd gotten that brown. Mum had not been happy either and had more than once complained about the sun that had permanently bleached out my once brownish head of hair. It was now blonde or streaked blonde, or what was left of it. Mum said it looked like corn silk, all streaky and shiny. But then, much as she said she didn't like to, her secret way of curing an illness was to chop off hair.

Hair, she said was known to sap one's strength. So, when I had the measles, she chopped it all off. She had chopped off the boy's hair too, but they didn't seem to mind! I think she thought that was what had saved my life. But think the truth was that she was happy not having to deal with my unruly head of hair. It was never going to be as ramrod straight as hers. Mine tended towards curls, just like Pa's, although his looked just fine. Mum kept hers in a tidy bun that was unlike what I had to comb through each day. Hers was always neat and orderly. It was much like how she kept her house and everything around her. Not like me, which she reminded me of all too often.

Now, after the slicing job that Mum had done to be sure my strength wasn't sapped, it was slowly growing back. Soon, I hoped, it would be long enough to tie back with a ribbon.

Anyhow, now she was on the mainland, and I was here. For a moment I had to wonder why I hadn't been brought there. She rushed my brothers off at the first sign of reddish bumps.

Regardless, if I didn't hustle, that corn wasn't going to do anyone a bit of good. Those flocks of geese that flew through this morning would think I set it out special just for them. But then I thought, was it safe to be out there? Should I be heading off on my own with what looked like the entire British Navy dropping anchor off our coast?

Caution wasn't part of my plan. Picking up my basket, I let the door slam behind me.

O THUS BE IT EVER...

It was hot. Well, not as hot as it can be in July or August but seemed too hot for the almost beginning days of autumn. The work was tiresome, and it truly was going to take most of the day to finish what must have easily been two acres of a nearly destroyed cornfield.

Already I had been to the barn twice to dump out the basket that overflowed. It was mostly horse corn as I was wont to call it. Well, I could call it whatever I liked, we weren't going to eat it, what with it already nearly dried out.

It was on the third trip that I remembered the wheelbarrow. One of the handles had broken off that Pa had said he'd repair. I guess I was the one who wasn't being careful and had snapped it off. He hadn't gotten to it yet what with all the other tasks that needed to be done. But there was enough left of the handle so's I could at least wheel it back and forth.

Pa of course used the wagon and old Gertie

when he needed to bring a load down to the dock. I wasn't allowed to hitch that old mare up on my own – T'isnt girl's work he'd said. So, I ended up hauling in all the crops on my own. No horse-drawn wagon for me. More than once I thought maybe I should wait for his return. But that could be days if he was being cautious. And who knew what would happen next if I didn't get it all in.

Too bad that older brother that I should have had didn't make it past his second birthday. He could've been doing all this work and I could have been sitting in the shade carding our flax or wool, or busy with some other task that wasn't so danged tiresome.

Actually, carding was one of my favorite chores as it took little effort to work with the two combs as they took out the bits and pieces of debris, leaving a soft pile of wool or flax. Then, of course, I'd get to spin it. Another favorite task as it involved sitting next to the fire, often on a chilly evening where I'd get to stay toasty warm. There also wasn't the constant threat of *get it done and get it done now.*

But Mum did lose her firstborn. It was a boy, and he was about two years old. They hardly spoke of it. Must have been sickness. Wasn't sure. It was before I was born and maybe that was why she was so firm about caring for me and being extra cautious. Like how she had insisted on chopping off my hair, which she was sure would make me well, and then rushing off to get the twins to a "proper" doctor.

Yes, they were twins. Not only did they look alike but they had the same wild streak, forever getting into mischief. Mum named them Thomas and George, after our presidents. They were hard to tell apart. They wouldn't answer anyway, no matter which name was used.

Regardless, they were extra cautious with those two. Guess it came from losing their firstborn. But Mum had no faith or trust in Doc Bailey. She said he learned all his doctoring by trial and error, and she didn't want to be part of his *error* group. She had hightailed it off to St. Michaels at the first sign of a red bump on George's chest.

"Off we go," she'd said, her dark eyes flashing that warning that said don't mess with her. She bundled them up in so many quilts they nearly disappeared. Pa was set to deliver his first load of tobacco anyway so sailed them over to the mainland. She was not going to lose another child. I did wonder sometimes why they hadn't rushed me off to the doctor!

But I needed to quit ruminating over things that were, or things that had been. Sometimes I just plain out wondered if anyone cared one bit about me. But it was time to stop whining, no one was listening anyhow and if I was to finish what I'd been tasked with I'd have to get moving.

"Get all that danged corn in," I said to no one in particular. "Damaged or not, can't leave it out here for the critters." My voice sounded strange in the great outdoors all by myself. But Pa had been firm when he sailed off to deliver Mum and the boys. He wanted those fields cleared. He said he'd be back as soon as he got the tobacco to market and Mum and my brothers settled. Who knew when that would be?

Anyhow, I was getting close to finishing up. The day had been clear, and already the sun was starting to dip below the horizon. I could hear the waves lapping at the shore. A puff of wind rattled the leaves in the trees and the dried stalks of corn. It was a calm day so there was little other sound – 'cept for my feet crunching on the blown-over stalks, and my talking to myself.

It was good that for the most part the cornfield had been nearly picked clean. There were still a few ears on the bent-over stalks, but it could wait. I'd rather start harvesting the flax, which was another of my chores. When it was picked and cleaned, I could begin carding it and then spinning it into thread. That at least was a crop the Brits had no interest in. Well so far anyhow. They probably wouldn't know what it was for anyway and I'd heard they were hungry more than anything else and it certainly couldn't be eaten.

It was already September, so evenings were cooling after the sun went down. It made it perfect for spinning. We used our flax for clothing. We didn't have a loom for the weaving part, but the Carlson's did. They lived in town. Well maybe most wouldn't call it a town but there was a shop, a livery stable, and a post office, so for this small island, we liked to call it a town. It was an easy walk, maybe a mite too long as I did prefer to ride Gertie. Pa would let me take her if I was on an errand. She was easy enough to ride although Mum said young ladies did not ride horses. I should be in the wagon. But she most often ignored it and let me go.

Anyhow, the Carlsons were very nice. They were alone with no kids but seemed to enjoy children. Children to them would be anyone under 20. Well at 15, I didn't feel like a child, but Mrs. Carlson was always so nice. She was very generous, both with warm cider in the winter and cool tea in the summer, always with a small sprig of mint, so I always enjoyed coming in to use her loom.

That loom took up a very large space in their home, so it was a good thing that it was there and that we didn't have to make room for one in our house. I was very good at stringing threads for her when she needed the help. Her fingers didn't work quite as well as mine or just weren't as long. I did notice though that when I hadn't finished the weaving that I'd been tasked with, she'd most often finish it for me. It was our secret. She never told Mum, although it may have been easy enough to see. Her weaving was so smooth, there were few bumps and tangles.

Mum always sent me with loaves of bread and cheese that we'd made as a gift for allowing us to share. And now, I was already looking forward to getting over there later in the fall. And if I had to spend all my days in this part of the world, on this far away island with nothing to do but chores, this was certainly one of the more pleasant things to do.

Nothing was terribly far away. The Island was maybe four miles long. I'd never actually walked the whole length and breadth of it. Maybe someday. It wasn't much to speak of when you compare it to the mainland, which went on forever. But it was nice enough for most who lived here. Well certainly not me, but for now I didn't know what else to do. I did know I wanted to get off this desolate and lonely piece of land and find a real life with people and adventures and fun. Would it ever happen for me I wondered for the hundredth time? Or was this to be my life forever. I kicked at a stone in the path trying to dislodge it. It didn't move. "Ouch." It looked like I was going to have a lump at the tip of my big toe.

HOME OF THE BRAVE…

For the hundredth time I wondered, would it ever be possible for me to leave this desolate piece of land? I'd passed all my grades before school let out this year. I had no need of further instruction. I could go to the mainland on my own – if they'd ever let me!

What I wanted was to maybe get up to New England and work in one of those factories that they're all talking about. That's where they were going to ship all their cotton and flax, and I wanted to be part of it. And they paid you to work there!

Not too long ago, Mum had said that I was skilled enough to become a dressmaker. I wasn't so sure about that. But it didn't matter. I really shouldn't even be thinking of these things as I know they wouldn't let me go anyway. All that way up to far off New England? Who'd tend to all the chores if I was no longer here?

Sometimes I wondered if they'd ever pondered what would happen if they didn't have me to do all the work. This piece of land would be impossible to keep up and Pa had no slaves. Guess he didn't really need any 'cause he had me. I did the work of ten people. Really, between the animals, the chickens, the cooking, the laundry, harvesting, taking care of the twins who were never where they were supposed to be, what would they do without me?

It was a pleasant enough thought. Leaving that is. I could travel towards the north, and maybe if not working in one of those factories, maybe a shop. I could sleep late and play for as long as I liked. Maybe I could even find a friend. I didn't really have any. There were very few girls my age on this godforsaken island. Janey was in town, but we were both kept so busy with chores that it was rare when we could get together. When we did, there was endless laughing or giggling at something funny we'd seen or heard. It was always so much fun to be with her.

But she worked in her family's general store, and they needed her all the time. She was after all the one who did most of the work. Her parents said it was good for her. I don't think she agreed but she most often did what she was told. She did get to talk with people all day and make as many friends as she wanted. Her job was to take care of the customers and keep the shop stocked with whatever her parents brought over from the mainland.

We did get to see each other in church on Sundays but that didn't always happen, what with all the demands on our time. We could never stay, always in a rush to get back to the farm. 'Course that just gave Mum's father, the Pastor, more reason not to like us.

But Janey was happy here, unlike me, but then she had eyes for Matthew. He was a waterman spending his days catching crabs or fish and sometimes tonging for oysters. He had a very small farm too and had trouble keeping up with everything. What with his entire family being lost on the Bay that night. That was the one time he didn't go with them. When they went to the mainland. And look what happened! And now that farm, it was all his to worry over and care for, and then the boat, his house and all the work that went with it.

It was sad, that's for sure. Losing his family. But I guess it can happen. Storms can come up out of nowhere especially when dark is coming on. Course they shouldn't have started out that late, but they did. They were coming back from the mainland on that little sloop they'd owned forever. Both of Matthew's sisters were in the boat as well as his Pa. His Mum had died years ago. Don't remember why she died. Anyhow, his Pa and sisters had gone over to try to market the linen that his two sisters had spent the entire winter weaving. And look what happened.

It was unfortunate 'cause those two girls knew what they were doing with a loom. They were so skilled they had even done embroidery on some of the linen and some they had dyed to wonderful colors. They'd used that indigo that was sold in Janey's shop. It certainly made for an interesting and different blue. But much of what they did was too special for everyday wear. It was meant for dress-up only, not anything that we'd ever wear on this island. But they made it over with their boat loaded with goods to trade and then never returned.

When Matthew went to the mainland to try to find them, he discovered that they had in fact sold all they had and traded for some things in St. Michaels. But exactly what had happened to them on their return, no one was ever to learn.

There had been a huge storm that had come

up the Bay late that day after they had sailed off from the mainland. Not too many days after, the boat had washed up on the shore. It'd lost its mast. But that's all they found.

Matthew's Pa knew of the treachery of the Bay and knew better than to set out when weather threatened. So, no one ever discovered what had become of them. All I know is that now Matthew and Janey are sweet on each other, and I also know Matthew could certainly use the help on his farm 'cause he's so often off fishing in the bay.

Some of the men on the island had gone over to his farm once or twice during the past year to help out. Pa had too, but heaven knows he had more than enough work on his own farm! And there I go again, ready to complain. But now remembering the fate of Matthew's family, I was becoming a bit concerned. Where was my family and why hadn't they returned?

The sun was setting, with streaks of gold shooting out in all directions. The waters were calm. There was a nice breeze so if they were on their way, travel should be easy. I certainly hoped they were on their way! It was lonely out here all by myself.

I'd been at my work long enough, daydreaming my way through my chores. Off in the distance, I could just make out two more ships, way down, towards the south. There were more this year than we'd ever seen. Always before there would be an occasional merchant ship that would head up to Baltimore, but not much else. 'Course all the watermen were out there every day chasing after the fish, or tonging for oysters, or pulling in crabs. But now there must be something unusual going on that was bringing all these ships into our Bay. And they were all British, anyhow as best I could tell.

I remembered the tales of last year when the Brits sailed up the Bay and attacked Havre de Grace. I didn't know much about that, but were they heading there again I wondered?

"This can't be good," I said. I said it out loud maybe just to hear the sound of a voice. It sure was getting lonely out here.

LAND OF THE FREE . . .

It was day three of everyone being gone. Except me.

Why was I the only one who was forever stuck on this Island? I had the measles too and Mum didn't rush me to the mainland.

Did anyone in the entire Chesapeake Bay care that I was tired, that I had blisters on my hands from that danged wheelbarrow? It was so wobbly it felt like it was going to collapse at any moment - along with me, I thought.

And there were blisters on my feet. I didn't even have decent boots. I had long ago outgrown Mum's cast-offs. There was the promise of new this fall but not sure if that would ever really happen.

The answer of course was to go barefoot and hope the few snakes that we had would be more interested in setting up their winter homes than chasing after one barefoot farm girl. Nevertheless, I was cautious. I'd heard of others not faring so well after meeting up with one of nature's mistakes. I didn't even want to remember that boy at school. He had been showing off and taunting one in the tall grasses. It really wasn't concealed and was rattling its tail in warning. That boy didn't do so well and forever more, or for as long as I knew him, he walked with a limp.

But those British ships were still there. Their masts clearly outlined on the horizon, their flags rippling in the breeze. Caution would be part of my plan for today, but then I had far too much to do to give them much attention, besides which, chances were slim that they'd come all this distance. We were way out on the end of the island, too far from where they were dropping anchor.

We'd heard tell that they'd pillaged a good bit of the fall harvest closer in, near town. Chances were they wouldn't bother us. What would they come for? Some spoiled corn or a few old hens?

The day began too early. It was all up to me, there was no one else to do it. So, I fed the chickens, collected the eggs, I only broke one — then brought fresh hay to the sheep, milked Flossie, and returned to the field to try to finish bringing in what remained of our corn. I was hungry too. I missed Mum's cooking. She was so much better at it than I would ever be. It was not my favorite thing to do, and I only worked with her in the kitchen now and again – when I had to. There was too much else to do. Now, the only thing I had found to eat were a few stale biscuits. It was too much to have to start cooking so I had eaten those along with a couple of our apples.

Some of the fields were cleared as Pa had taken in the last of our tobacco. He'd done the curing and was already carrying it off to market. We didn't use much land for it although Pa said it was worth good money. It took everything out of the soil that did any good for anything else. It made it hard to grow other crops, so he felt it was best to rotate what we planted.

This year we had put corn in most of the fields. At least our livestock could eat the corn. So could we if it hadn't all been knocked down by the storm. The only thing we could do with tobacco was sell it on the mainland. Couldn't eat it! And it took some effort to harvest, then cure it.

And then, just when I was truly tired of talking to myself, there was Rip. Now as any girl on the entire island would agree, he could be the worst tease and pest in the entire world, and he was to be avoided. However, on this day, although hard to believe, he had actually come by to help. He tended to do that now and again for no good reason that I could ever understand. But there he was. And I should be thankful, but I was about done for the day.

No one that I'd ever heard of had ever given much consideration to where this boy actually lived. If we'd even thought about it, we probably would have guessed it was in someone's barn. More'n likely different barns as he wasn't one to stay still. People fed him now and again and gave him hand-me-down clothes. In return he would help with the crops or unload a wagon or haul some water. We assumed he was a freed black slave, but good sense said, more than likely he was a runaway. The slash marks on his legs and arms, now well healed over, told of a life that hadn't always been so carefree.

We'd all heard the story of how the watermen found him clinging to a piece of driftwood, near death, much of his flesh ripped open. Probably by a whip but no one liked to talk of such things. But that's where the name came from. Rip. When the watermen talked about him, they'd always say remember the kid with the ripped-up legs!

He never corrected them or shared his real name or ever said anything about his past and no one that I know of ever questioned him too closely. Easier to just accept what was here. With no effort that I ever noticed, he slipped into becoming a member of our small community. Some adults actually liked him. Well, 'cept people like me and Janey. We found him to be a constant annoyance, much like the two little brothers that I already had.

But there he was. Some felt that he was likable enough as he would often appear just when another set of hands was most needed. Well, he helped mostly adults. To me, he was always more of an aggravation regardless that he would often pitch in. Janey and I saw him as no more than a pesky vexation no matter how much he helped.

And, if we even cared, we suspected he had as much schooling as we'd had. Most days he could be found sitting under the window of our schoolhouse. He was listening to the same teaching that we listened to. He had in fact even dared to ask us questions now and again after a day's lessons.

Geography seemed to be his favorite subject as he'd ask where this or that country was located and where was our navy and did we really control the seas. To that we answered no - the Brits did. We knew that much. They had far more ships than we did, which really didn't concern us – well except when they were anchored off our very shore. But the sea seemed to fascinate him. Maybe he wanted to be a sailor. I wasn't sure and didn't ask.

"Ya' want help," he asked. He knew I was out here alone 'cause he knew everyone's business.

This day had been far too long, with endless work. But "nope," I answered. It really was too late, and I didn't want to get started with anything else. "I'm done," I said, wiping the drips off my forehead. "Heading in."

He turned away and kicked at a stone with his barefoot. I heard a quiet "ouch!" He was probably going to sleep in our barn. I didn't care but I didn't want to offer him food or anything, lord knows then he'd never go away. I didn't even know what I was going to eat.

I was ready to go in for the night. And then looked out again. Those Brits were still out there. They were anchored right off the shore, close to town. And if my eyes weren't deceiving me, it looked like even more to the south of our island were heading this way. This was not good; I was sure of that. Didn't we have our independence? We'd won it from England years ago. It had been settled by the Revolutionary War. We all learned about it in school. So why were they here now and did it have anything to do with their burning down Washington? And was this really our second war for independence? Well, that's what Pa called it. The first war for independence was near 40 years ago.

And did they really burn down Washington? I wasn't sure about that, but someone coming from the mainland said that they'd burned most of that city just a few days ago. That was before Mum left with the boys, and her only comment was that you can't trust every bit of gossip that people want to share. But this was so odd. I wished Pa would come home.

It was very near dusk. I'd completed most of my chores. The chickens were starting to settle in for the night. The sheep were bedding down and even that old hooty owl was starting to make his evening calls. And the bats, so reliable as the sun made its way below the horizon, were darting about catching the last of the summer bugs.

I was trying to decide if it was worth going to the far field to bring in the last of those collard greens. Who likes collard greens anyhow I thought? Well, Mum does, I guess. It just wasn't one of my favorites. They could be boiled up for my dinner, but really it was too much trouble for something I wasn't fond of anyway.

"Leave them," I said out loud. "I'll get them tomorrow."

I really wasn't paying much attention to anything except threading my way back thru the last of the cornstalks and trying to be aware that there could be snakes and not trip over the broken stalks. Then I thought I heard Rip's favorite bird call. He'd do that now and again. It was sort of like a distant mourning dove, low and sort of sad. It was his favorite bird. I turned to look to determine if it was actually a bird or if it was Rip teasing me - again. He was never going to teach me how to do it. I knew that much. Girls can't whistle he said.

And then, from out of nowhere, and I mean nowhere as I'd heard and seen nothing, a large grimy hand slapped over my mouth.

It was just like that. I hadn't seen anyone. Or heard anything.

How could this have happened?

Who was this?

Why hadn't I been more attentive?

The hand wouldn't allow a scream.

A burly, hairy arm nearly crushed my bones as I was lifted into the air and thrown over some monster's shoulder.

I tried to turn to see who was holding me. I tried to scream. It was impossible. I couldn't even move. His footsteps crushed the stalks of corn still lying in the field. His grip was tight, I nearly couldn't breathe. For a moment I was sure I caught a glimpse of Rip back in the tall grasses. I looked again and there was no one.

That's all I remember.

FITFULLY BLOWS...

It was dark. Where was I? How'd I get here?

My eyes didn't want to adjust, they just wanted to stay shut. Maybe I could disappear. Maybe I was dreaming. Maybe this wasn't really happening.

Water was lapping, like waves splashing on a boat. My hands and feet were tied with string. Not very securely. Should I break free? And if I did, where would I go? Where was I?

I didn't want to know! But with incredible clarity, I knew where I was. Good grief. How could this have happened?

The floor I was curled up on was swaying. A gentle sort of back and forth. The scent in the air was of damp wood and mustiness. This couldn't be. How had this happened?

A gag was tied around my mouth. Too tight but there was nothing I could do. The darkness was cold and unfriendly - and lonely. Footsteps were passing overhead.

That's all I remembered before falling into a troubled sleep. The gentle rhythm of the waves should have been calming.

~

"Git up." It was the angry voice of whoever was attached to the boot kicking my side. "Now," it yelled. "I ain't sayin' it again."

Rubbing at my eyes, with the string digging into my wrists, I tried to remember where I was. And why? Was this a dream? What had happened?

The boot kicked at my side again. "Git yerself up boy or yer gonna feel the sting o' my whip."

Boy? Was he talking to me?

"Good Lawd," the voice said. "Do dey really have to gag an' tie ye? Said they'd find me someone. Humph," he said as he slipped a knife under the ties. "Didn't want a kid. Was hopin' for someone bigger."

I'm not a kid I wanted to say, I'm almost as tall as my Pa! I pulled the rag away from my mouth. Long fingers grabbed my arm and forced me to my feet.

"Why'd they a'ways have to do it this way?"

He shook his head back and forth.

"Well, ye be mine now."

"Dis way," he said, dropping me. My legs were unsteady. I wasn't sure if I could follow him. The floor was also rocking. How could that be?

"In there," he said. His grimy thumb pointed to a small room.

My eyes were having trouble focusing. My feet were having trouble directing me. My legs felt as though they were going to collapse under me. He shoved me into a tight little room.

I rubbed at my eyes trying to focus. The voice said. "Chop 'em up, and don't let no seeds get in 'em. And don't dare give me trouble or you's gonna end up like dat last one."

What? What was he saying? What last one?

"There," he said, "Git them apples chopped and do it now." He didn't have to yell. The room wasn't very large, and his voice bounced off the walls.

"Uhh," was all that came out.

"There's the knife. There's the pot. There be them apples." He spoke to me as though he was speaking to a very young child.

Trying to understand where I was and exactly what had happened, I reached out for the knife. My head wasn't working. There was a sudden, sharp stinging. Drops of blood were falling from my fingers. I'd picked up the wrong end of the knife.

"Are ye daft boy?" he asked.

Tears were threatening. Don't I said to myself. Do as he says. There'll be more trouble for sure if I fall into a heap of tears or worse if I get sassy.

A rag hung near the door. It would stop the drops of blood.

I picked up the handle of the knife, this time the right end. I didn't cut myself. The apples looked fresh and were easy to core and cut up.

The room was hot and close. The chopping took longer than it should have but I was still baffled and trying to understand what had happened and why.

"Where am I?" I asked. My voice was raspy. I'd gotten through most of the basket of apples. I didn't want to aggravate the bearded, bearlike body that was taking up most of the space.

"What're ya talkin' about boy?" he asked. "Ye're daft ain't ya." It wasn't a question.

I wanted to stamp my foot and say, no I'm not daft and I'm certainly not a boy. But I held my tongue.

"Yer on the good ship HMS Tonnant" he answered and none too kindly. "Where'd ya think you was at?"

Was I really on a ship? And a British ship at that! I just shook my head and went back to peeling and chopping.

"Ain't you never been on a ship 'fore?" he asked. It didn't sound like a real question, so I let it go as he continued to talk. "Heard they was gonna' find more help," he said. "And lookie what they come up with? A boy just fresh outa' his nappies."

He thought that was particularly funny and let out a noise, which could have been a laugh. "What's yer name boy? Ever served in a galley before?" he asked.

I was quite sure he was an American. He had a drawl that spoke of the deep south. It lacked the formality of the English accent. Was he another kidnapped seaman? Impressed they called it, but it wasn't for me to question.

I kept my head down and shook my head and answered "no."

"Well then, this be yer lucky day. We be headin' out soon's they can. Think it be Bal'imore. But no tellin' after that mess in Washin'ton."

Too much to try to understand. Where do I start? He thinks I'm a boy. Well, that could be a good thing, but I certainly didn't think I looked like one, but then I looked down at the trousers that were too big for me. I had rolled them up some and I was barefoot. I had Pa's old linen shirt on. But worst or maybe best of all – the short haircut that Mum insisted on when I'd been sick with the measles. So maybe this wasn't so bad. I did know that girls didn't fare well in the hands of soldiers or sailors.

I'd been kidnapped. I started to shake. Impressed they called it. This was not so unusual. We'd all heard of it. It had happened before when the British had ships going up the Chesapeake, but not on our island, not that I'd ever heard of. I'd seen the ships heading up the Bay, but we were supposed to be safely tucked away on the remote end of the island. And now here I was. And worst of all, who would even know I was gone?

Well maybe Rip. I may have seen him in the tall marsh grass or heard him just before whatever monster it was that had grabbed me. But had it been him?

Pa hadn't come home. There was nobody there and our cow needed to be milked and the chickens were loose, and I hadn't finished bringing in the corn or the flax. How would anyone know?

"Snap it up there now. We're about due to be serving the meal and them officers don't tolerate any sloppiness from the galley. Well, not my galley anyways. Git them apples in the stew pot."

The accent was not English. But from where? I dared not ask.

He was stirring a huge steaming pot of oatmeal. He was cooking it way longer than it needed. It was turning to mush. It smelled like it was burning too. But not for me to say!

He ladled the lumpy mess into the line of bowls set out in an almost neat row. "There it be," he said. "Get'm all out to them tables now or we're gonna be in big trouble. And stir them apples s'more. Don't want mush. Just warmed and softened. That be how they likes 'em."

I stirred the apples, plopped a spoonful on each bowl of oatmeal. He pointed to the tables. "Set 'em out there. Be neat about it."

As best I could I placed a filled bowl at each place. There was already a tankard and a cup, and a napkin in a brass ring set out. I'd put the last of the steaming bowls down, as they began to file in and take their seats. It was a group of men, some looked like boys, all wearing similar uniforms. Most were tall and all as thin as reeds in a springtime marsh. Most were rubbing sleep out of their eyes. They seemed to know what they were about, each taking a place at the two long tables. I wasn't noticed except for the demand for more biscuits.

It took many trips back and forth to the galley to get them all served. There were lots more apples and I poured them into large serving bowls with silver ladles and plopped one down on each table. They were heavy and they were hot.

Tea needed to be poured and the tankards filled with a rum and water mixture. Too early in the morning, I thought for strong liquor. But then the cook said, "Makes for a better drink, ... case the waters bad."

The serving went on for an hour. Plates to clear, tankards to fill, serving dishes to be removed and refilled. There was laughter and then serious talk that seemed to quiet whenever I entered. I heard the words Baltimore, Washington, cannons, and war. I kept my head down and tried to look as though I wasn't listening to all their chatter.

Cook was after me every minute. He continued with his tirade: "Why'd I let the tankards run out of grog?" "How come I wasn't keeping up with the bread baskets." "Had I mopped up the spill?"

It was endless. When the last of the diners threw down his napkin and left, I thought my legs would collapse beneath me.

There was little food left and now the pile of dirty plates would have to be cleaned.

Why was I here and was this to be my life forevermore? How would I ever get out of this? I wanted to go home.

THE TERROR OF FLIGHT...

My day was filled with time in the galley. We cooked for the entire ship and Cook thought I should be the one to tend to the Officer's Mess.

Mess? Well, that's what he called it; I have no idea why. Of course, my thought was that they'd made such a mess – therefore the name!

And then there was a boy, somewhat younger than me. He was so busy tending to all the others that I hardly saw him. In his dining area the sailors ate in shifts, so as soon as he was done with one seating, the next group would arrive. He needed lots more help. It was near impossible to keep up. But I wasn't the one who could step in. I'm quite sure my feet had blisters on top of blisters from running back and forth from my tables to the kitchen, or galley as they were wont to call it.

When the breakfast clean-up was done and Cook wasn't paying me any attention, I slipped out. This was most assuredly a large ship, and I was sure we were still at anchor. For a moment I wondered if the plan was to sail to England. Was this impressment? Just like what Pa had gone through? How would I get word to Mum? How would I get off this ship?

It took moments only to get up to the main deck where everyone appeared to be busy. Each seemed to have a job, giving their attention to one task or another. One gnarled old sailor was mending a sail with an oversized needle. Another was cleaning the deck with a raggedy and much-used mop. Others had climbed up the mast and were working with ropes. They all seemed absorbed in their task.

We were anchored and I was sure I could see my island in the distance. I was also certain that I could see Matthew's sailboat way off-shore. His sails were different colors, so it wasn't hard to pick him out. The mainsail was very old, and the jib, maybe not so old was a faded dark color with more than a few patches.

He never much cared what color they were or how many patches had to be sewn on, as long as they worked. I think my friend Janey had something to do with mending some of those rips and tears.

He was probably busy with his fishing as it

appeared that he was cruising along the shore. It wasn't hard to see that he was keeping his distance from the big ships. I wondered if I jumped overboard could I swim towards shore? Could I get Matthew's attention and if I did, would he sail to me? Would we both be shot? I wished I could've waved or let him know where I was, but I didn't know how, and he was so far away. What if they caught me signaling him, then what?

But I'd been gone too long. I hustled back down to the galley hoping Cook had been busy with other things and hadn't noticed my absence. I wondered what sort of punishment there was if one didn't tend to their work.

I hadn't meant to be gone so long and arrived back just as he was lugging in a huge mess of crabs. "They catch 'em last time dey was ashore," he said. I nodded and was glad he didn't make note of my long absence.

He said *they* had caught the crabs. I wondered who "they," were. I doubted that it could have been any of the sailors on board as few people outside of our area had any idea about eating crabs. I suspected that they'd probably stolen them from one of the watermen. Few people from away knew of our tasty treat and how delectable they could be. It was our secret and here were all these British sailors thinking they knew what to do with them. How could they? It was a local food source that few outsiders knew about.

But there was too much to do, and I needed to get to work. It took the rest of the morning just to finish cleaning and getting the tables set up and the bread made. I still wasn't sure of my role here other than to do as I was told.

And then Cook wasn't preparing the crabs properly! But it wasn't up to me to correct him. He just threw them all into a huge kettle of boiling water and let them boil away. Far too long but not my place to comment on the skills of a cook who was sure he knew everything.

Using long tongs, he pulled them out, one at a time. They didn't look very appetizing, but he heaped them on platters. The red color, now an overcooked pink, did make for a nice look all piled up.

The bongs sounded and again one by one they arrived at the mess. I had to scurry to bring the overfilled platters to the tables. Some of the diners smiled and others looked a bit perplexed as though they weren't too sure what to do with a steaming pile of what should be a delectable treat. The fellow at the end of the table with a bushy mustache picked one up and turned it over and over, playing with the claws and looking totally perplexed.

No one asked. But I took up one of the crabs and pulled back the shell. I cracked the claws with the handle of a knife and pulled out the meat. They were way overcooked, but how would these strangers know? I suspected they'd never even seen a crab before, much less eaten one. They did all seem to enjoy them. They were actually laughing as they cracked the shells. I saw a few fingers that were bloodied by not taking care. But they chuckled and kept at it.

'Course they had to fill up on bread and potatoes as a pile of overcooked crabs wasn't going to satisfy their hungry appetites.

The meal was done. It was late and I hadn't finished the cleanup. From the wooden mugs to the trenchers and platters that held their meal, to the pots that Cook insisted I should clean. It was endless. And with the boat swaying back and forth, I thought maybe I was going to be sick.

It took forever, but then I took the pile of empty shells and dumped them back where they came from - over the side and into the Bay. My job really wasn't finished but I knew I'd be sick if I went below deck again.

Trying to look as though I had a mission or a job, I walked along the deck with some determination. The air was good, away from the smells of cooking foods. A couple of the seamen were eyeing me with curiosity. Too much curiosity I thought. It was time to disappear.

Dropping down the hatchway to below decks I discovered an entire area where it appeared everyone had a berth or a hammock. Except me. It didn't matter.

Exhaustion caught up with me. I curled up in a very small hammock tucked back in a corner. It was hardly big enough so no doubt it didn't belong to anyone. There was an itchy wool blanket that appeared to be unclaimed and a burlap sack that would work for a pillow. I was ignored. It was good.

My eyes were closed tight even before I'd gotten comfortable. It was hard not to be lulled to sleep. The ship's gentle rocking felt much like being in the hammock Pa had strung between our two old apple trees. Homesickness swept over me.

NO REFUGE COULD SAVE
THE HIRELING AND SLAVE...

Pa would have known what all this was about. He had worked on a merchant ship once – well that was until he'd been impressed by the Brits. He rarely spoke of it – but back in school, we learned that Americans being impressed into the British Navy may well have been what started this war. The war we were now fighting.

It had been going on for two years what with the Brits invading all of America along the coast. Guess our independence hadn't settled with them yet!

But they had even been up in Canada. It was a war that was now even threatening our quiet little island. Too often we saw their ships sailing up and down the Bay. It was a bit disconcerting. And then it wasn't more than a couple of years ago, when a group of warships, sailed past, their cannons protruding from the wooden sides of the ships. It was said they had sailed all the way up to Havre de Grace, way up at the top of the Bay - and there'd been a battle. But I'd never been there so I wasn't sure what that was all about.

And as for Pa being captured? He rarely ever spoke of it. But we did know that he had been made to serve on a ship with the Brits. Last winter, on a night when he was particularly comfortable, with his feet stretched out toasting in the warmth from the hearth, he told us some of the tale of his escape. He tried to make light of it in the telling.

He said he'd used his wits to get away from the Brits. He said that with two other Americans, he had jumped overboard, in the dark of night. He said they nearly drowned but the three made their way over to a small skiff that had been tied up to the back of the big ship. They shouldn't have been towing that boat he said. It should have been brought back on board. It was trailing behind and no one had taken any notice.

The three were in luck. They cut the rope and they were free. It was in the dead of night somewhere off the coast of New England. They rowed to shore, which he said wasn't all that far. They could just make it out in the moonlight.

Knowing how to swim he said had saved his life. That was no doubt why he had taught all of us how to swim. It was probably before we could walk – well anyhow I can't remember a day when I didn't know how. But he felt it was that important. It had already saved his life. And we lived on an island, so it did make sense. And if truth be known, on a hot summer day, there was nothing better than jumping into the cool Bay waters.

Pa said he had always loved the sea, but after being captured for so long, he had no desire to return. He had also become extremely distrustful of almost all humans. That was why he decided he wanted to live out his days alone. He ended up on Poplar Island! My home for my entire life.

He had no plans of ever leaving and had built a home way out on the end of the island so's not to be bothered by anyone. But then thankfully, the island had a preacher, and that preacher had a daughter. That daughter caught my Pa's eye and that's where my brothers and I came from.

Something was rubbing on my face. It was

soft. It felt like fur. I didn't want to open my eyes. I remembered what had happened and would be happy to never open my eyes again. I silently prayed that whatever it was, it would go away. I didn't even want to think if it was one of those rodents that we were forever chasing out of the chicken's shed. Don't move I thought and maybe it'll go away.

There was a quiet meow and a cool dry nose that was busy sniffing at me. I did not want to wake up, but I peeked from one half-opened eye. There standing on my chest, looking down at me was a fluff ball of grey. She had whiskers sticking out of each side of a small and curious face. "Well now, what are you doing here?" I whispered. There was relief in my voice, I'm sure.

And just as I was about to reach out to my new friend, the toe of a large leather boot poked my side.

"Up with ye now. Don't be sleeping the day away."

I rubbed at my eyes and looked up into the face of the cook. His overly hairy eyebrows were squinched together, forming a bushy grey line. I knew I should not be caught lying down. I knew there were still platters and bowls and tankards that were stacked up waiting to be cleaned. I remembered nearly fainting away from tiredness and then sneaking off. It must have occurred to him at some point that I was no longer there.

"Git on back in that galley 'fore I have ya flogged," he said. "Yer jus' like the last one. Ha!" he added. "He didn't las' long neither."

I must have looked perplexed. "Picked him up down south somewheres, we did. Grabbed him on our way out of port. Needed the help." That's as much as I heard. A wooden spoon was poking out of one hand. He was glaring at me.

"Do ye 'spose we're all takin' the day to lollygag?" He asked. His voice was filled with mockery.

I very nearly fell out of the hammock, forgetting where I was. "Git back in there. There's them taters to peel and onions to skin and get that barrel o' meat goin'" he said. How're we gonna feed these here sailors if you sleep the whole day away? Tell me that now would ya?"

Scrambling out of the hammock, I upset my new furry companion. She jumped down and scurried off into a corner. I wanted to chase after her, she seemed so free.

"What're ya doin' with that danged cat?" He

asked. He shook his head. "Leave 'em be. He's got his job to do jus' like ya got yer job to do." He scowled and turned to stomp back to his galley.

I followed him, careful to stay out of reach. No telling what he'd do with that long wooden spoon that he kept slapping against his leg.

The galley was all steamy. "Over there," he said pointing to the bushel of onions. "Get 'em peeled and chopped and be quick about it."

From what I'd seen earlier, this was a very big ship. I knew that much. The smell of the sea was in every board and fiber. The floor rocked ever so gently beneath my feet. I worked quickly.

A young boy was there too. He had little to say but sounded like an American. He was busy stirring a huge pot filled with what may have been stew. He was the same one that I'd seen darting about before. I was reluctant to ask if he too had been captured but there was too much to do so I just kept peeling and chopping.

"Pullin' anchor tomorrow?" he asked. He was rifling around trying to find more serving pieces.

"Dat's not for us to guess," answered the cook.

"Well," said the young boy, "Heard them

talkin' in the other mess earlier, said they'd be headin' up the Bay. That's what was said. You don' have to believe me."

"Well keep yer chatter to yer'self," said the cook. "Whatever ye hear in the mess is not fer yer ears. We hear nothin'. Ye hear me?"

"Aw well," said the boy, not ready to let it go, "Near as I can tell, it won't be long. They got them canons cleaned and ready and saw 'em stackin' up more of them cannonballs."

Cook pretended he wasn't listening and scowled. That was when we heard the soft bong to announce the meal. Well, it wasn't quite ready, regardless of the bong! Most of the rest of the conversation was lost in the hustle to finish the preparation and then get it out there to the long tables before all the crew had taken their seats.

Cook didn't stop. He gave me one order after another – slice the bread, get it in the baskets, where's the spoons, didn't I have their tea ready? I tried to keep up but still felt lost while trying to find everything. The boy knew much more than I did and grabbed this and that and set it in front of me. He was quick and efficient, and I needed the help.

I could see all the hungry men taking their

seats. With luck, I had placed each of the cloth napkins back in the correct napkin holders and at the seat where I'd found them. Napkins, I had been informed, were always reused on long journeys. I didn't ask how and when they were washed.

But it was endless. Huge bowls of stew, endless bread and butter and cheese, and they ate what could have been a bushel of cut-up apples and fresh grapes. I suspected it all had been taken from our island!

I was carefully balancing a large bowl of stew when I slipped and nearly fell. I thought surely I was going to drop the bowl as some of the hot liquid spilled over my fingers – the fingers I had so recently sliced open! Part of the steaming brew ended up on the pant leg of one of the officers.

I was horrified.

Words wouldn't come. I couldn't speak.

"What?" he said and turned to me and although I could see surprise and maybe pain in his face, he shook his head and maybe bit back words he would've liked to have said. Instead, he sucked in his breath and said, "It's fine. I'll tend to it." He was an American, that much I could tell.

Two of the other officers snickered. I didn't know what to say so turned and headed back into the galley.

The boy found it very amusing, snickering a bit, but took over for me. He saw my distress and gave me a look, then shook his head that he wouldn't be sharing my mishap with the cook.

I got busy with the pail with dirty water and began the washing up of the same dishes that I'd cleaned earlier.

The boy was keeping up with serving both mess halls. He certainly knew what he was about. Cook continued to fill bowls and plates. We were close to having nothing left. But then napkins were thrown down, benches scrapped back, and they departed.

The boy came in and began to put away the cleaned dishes. "Thank you," I said, my words meant only for him. "Tell me your name."

"Name's Gerard," he answered. "But they calls me Boy." He shrugged his shoulders.

"Where are you from?" I asked.

"Everywhere. Nowhere." That wasn't any kind of answer. No doubt he was kidnapped from some coastal town. He had none of the British accent. But he had nothing more to offer.

The galley was close to being tidied up when there was a scampering of feet above. Orders were being yelled back and forth.

"What is happening?" I asked.

"Ah, they's pullin' anchor already." It was a statement from Cook.

"Where are they going?" I asked. I bit my lip willing the tears not to come.

"Who knows." It was Cook again, who then disappeared into the bowels of the ship.

Where were they going? Were they sailing for England? Why didn't he know? How would I get home? This can't be.

THE WAR'S DESOLATION...

"Boy," said Cook, pointing at me. "Git this cleaning up finished. It's yer job. Yer slow as molasses on a frozen pile 'o beans. Git it done now." He was pointing to the wooden table that had cheese and butter and fatback smeared all over it.

"Yes Sir," I said, using the only term I knew.

"I'm the cook boy, not one of yer officers. Name's Cook. Don't forget it. Ye got that?"

Of course, I thought, how could I not. He was a towering giant who took up most of the space in the galley. He was always stirring something or chopping something or slurping something and he was more often than not an untidy mess!

"What's yer name?" he barked. He must have been hard of hearing 'cause he yelled everything and most answers I gave had to be repeated. He also must have tired of calling both of us "Boy."

"Mackenzie," I answered, this time using a loud voice.

He heard me and looked at me. "That's no kind of name." He started eyeing me a bit too closely.

"Mac," I said. "It's Mac, short for Mackenzie." That's all I could think of. "Family name," I added.

That seemed more acceptable to him. "Well then Mac," he said, "if that's what yer really called, you and the other one git this here galley shining and git it done now."

I said something dumb under my breath, which thankfully he didn't hear. He left. There was lots more room when his bulk wasn't squeezed into every inch of space. The other boy was there and looking as annoyed as I was. But we both started in. It'd be short work if we both stayed with it.

"Hey Gerard," I said, while trying to dry and stack the endless bowls, "Are you from the Island?" I really didn't think so as I'd never seen him before, and we knew most everyone who lived there.

He spoke in a hushed voice. "What Island?" he asked.

"Why Poplar Island," I said. "And where'd you get the name Gerard," I asked.

"Don't know no Poplar Island," he answered. "And I made up my own name. It's a good one 'cause I don't know no one else by dat name."

He was cleaning deep inside one of the black iron pots and his voice was almost an echo.

"I'm from Poplar," I said. "Poplar Island," I added. "Didn't think I'd seen you before. Where are you from?"

Our voices were low as I learned he'd been in Washington D.C. when he was snatched from the dock area.

"I went down to find food from the stalls," he said, "Down by the waterfront. They throw out their bad food, which isn't always so bad." He was younger than me, and almost looked like he was enjoying a whole new adventure.

"What happened in Washington?" I asked, not believing what I'd heard, which I was sure wasn't true.

"It was huge," he answered shaking his head, his long hair sweeping into his eyes.

"What was huge?" I asked.

"Everything! The smoke, the soldiers, the fire, and everyone running. And noise! The booms from the cannons made my ears hurt.

And the gunshots!" He almost smiled. "The city was on fire."

So, it was true!

He wasn't done! "And then when it was as bad as it can get – there was a huge," he paused, "huge," he said again, "storm like I never seen before."

"What do you mean."

"There was thunder. There was lightenin'. There was one of them what d'ya call 'ems," he paused for a moment. "Ternados," he said. He was almost wiggling with excitement as he told the tale. "I saw it comin,'" he said. "Sky was as dark as it can get, like middle of the night dark. And dis thing snaked down from the clouds. Someone said run and that's when I hid."

"Never seen anything like that before," he said. "But it sure put out them fires. It also blew everythin' to bits." He was smiling, enjoying the telling. Then he added, "I'm thinkin' that's when the Brits decided to hightail it outa there." He had half a smile. "Dat's when they grabbed me."

"Well, where are your people?" I asked. "Do they know you're here?" Guess that was not a very good question for someone who'd been kidnapped.

"Got no people," he answered. He was wringing out the incredibly dirty rag that he'd been using to wipe down the kettles.

"Whyn't you have people," I asked. "Everyone has people."

"Nope, some of us don'," he answered. "Don' know as I ever had people. People if yer meanin' family."

I nodded as I wasn't sure I understood.

"Lived on them streets, most of my life. It was an o.k. life," he answered, "and I'm none to upset 'cause now I'm on a big ship heading to someplace else."

Really, I wanted to say but chose to be silent.

"Nothin' wrong wit' this life," he said. "I gets all the food I want and if I stay out of the way, they cain't come up with too much work for me to do. And look, we're off on another grand journey." He threw down his rag, "I'm gonna go see where we's headed." And with that, he left the galley.

I wasn't sure if he was sincere or just trying my patience. He was a curious one to be sure.

There was little else to do. I needed to get the last of the pots back in their place and then go on deck to have a look around and maybe determine where we were headed. With luck, no one would give me any attention.

There was no doubt that we were underway. I could feel the gentle swaying as we cut through the waves and heard the creaking of the old timbers as they settled into the gentle roll. The waters were calm making for an easy passage through the Bay waters. I could hear the slap of the canvas against the yardarms. I needed to get up there to see just where we were and where we were headed.

It took moments only to get up on deck. The sun was settling for the evening, and I watched as our shoreline disappeared in the distance. I felt a moment of terror. How would I ever get home? Was this to be my life? If I dove over the side, would I be able to swim all the way to shore? Would they shoot me? Fear like a tight blanket wrapped around me.

What was I to do? I had little experience on the water other than our small sloop. We used it when we needed to get to the mainland. 'Course I'd seen any number of ships heading up and down the Bay, probably merchant ships and most probably bound for Baltimore. But I'd never been on one. And this one was without a doubt huge. It was sailing under a British flag.

It was what we'd seen for the past week anchored off our shore.

Orders were being shouted back and forth. Everyone was busy with some task or other. The crew sounded as if they were from everywhere – from all around the world. Guess what Pa had said was true – seamen were impressed into the British service wherever and however they could find them. But I did not want to be one of them.

We were headed north; I could tell that much. My island was disappearing on the southern horizon. I didn't want to be here. How would I ever get home?

MORNING'S FIRST BEAM ...

This ship was big. Huge if it was compared to the little boats our watermen used. It most assuredly had been one that had been anchored off our shore. And there were more than a dozen others sailing along with us. Maybe it was the entire fleet that we'd seen earlier. I wasn't sure.

They had their sails full out. All taut and filled with the wind! What a sight. It was magnificent. Orders were being yelled back and forth. "Grab the line." "Secure that sail." "Mind the halyard."

And then "Git outa da' way boy. Cain't ya see we's busy." This came from a very dark African. He was hard to understand but he had on the same outfit as the others. He grabbed a line and continued on down the deck.

"They're not all from England, are they?" I asked or actually made a statement. I was standing next to a grizzled old barefoot sailor who seemed intent on repairing some roping.

"Good Lawd no." He laughed. Well, not a real laugh, more of just making mumbling noises from deep in his throat. "They be from ev'ywhere," he said. "Name a country. We got a sailor from there. They's impressed." He said to answer the question before I'd even asked. "Impressed boy," he said. "Tis another word for kidnapped." With this he laughed at his own attempt at humor.

I knew what impressed meant. That's what'd happened to Pa years ago. And now, I think that's what's happened to me.

"Been all over da world," he said as he continued with what looked like braiding a frayed rope.

"Seen battle up to Canada and down into the Car'bean. Was over 'round Europe for a spell but then they caught that danged Napoleon, and it was off to dis' place." He stopped long enough to wipe his nose on an already much-soiled sleeve.

"And just lookie here," he said as his gnarled and knobby fingers continued to braid. "We's headed up to Bawl'imore to finish the job."

Finish what job? I didn't say it out loud. I didn't really want the answer.

The rope he was braiding had been coiled but was now in a mess of snarls as he tried to repair it. I rose to leave when my foot caught in the tangle.

"What in tarnation ya' doin' boy," he yelled. He grabbed my arm. "Look what ya' done." He reached back to slap me. My cap came off and curls sprang free.

"Now what have we here? Percy are you grabbing the young boys again. What're we gonna do with you?" It was an officer, and he was eyeing me as though he was trying to figure something out.

"Unhand him," he said. And just like that, the old sailor released my arm, almost as if he were touching a hot coal.

I bent and grabbed my hat pulling it low. My hair was matted and dirty, but I tucked all the escaped curls behind my ears.

"Now," said the voice coming from the very tall man. "Are you doing your job or just letting that tongue wag?" I tried to duck even lower, hoping he wouldn't recognize me.

He was an American, I could tell that much. But he was also the one who I'd spilled stew on earlier. Oh Lord, I thought, is there a way that I can just disappear?

But there I was. He had a funny way of speaking. Maybe from New England. It was the same accent that the postmistress back in St. Michaels had. It was kind of amusing trying to understand her.

The gnarled old seaman ducked his head and said, "I's workin' Sir." His fingers continued their practiced and skilled braiding.

"Well then stick with it and mind your gossip."

"And you boy, shouldn't you be busy with something?"

"Yes Sir," I said. I didn't want to be questioned and he was looking at me oddly. I wasn't sure just what would happen, so pulled my hat even lower and turned to leave.

He followed me, then put a hand on my arm. "A moment, if you please," he said. He was inspecting me a bit too closely.

"Have I seen you before?" he asked. His accent definitely spoke of the north, not the proper English that the British liked to claim.

"No Sir," I answered looking at my bare toes.

"You're sure?"

His eyes were dark blue and very penetrating.

I pulled my shirt closer around my neck. I remembered yesterday's accident only too well.

"Ahhh," he said and nodded. "Stew!"

I could see a sort of half-smile. He lowered his voice, "Not sure exactly what's happening here or why you're on this ship." He looked more closely, "but you do work in the galley do you not?"

Words wouldn't come. I looked at my feet and tried to disappear. Tears were threatening.

The ship lurched. I lost my footing.

"Here now," he said. His hand gripped my elbow. "We should no doubt chat."

I looked up and met his eyes for a moment. I think my heart skipped a beat. His eyes were blue and so penetrating with what looked like merriment in the corners.

"Not now," he said. "Too much happening." He let go of my arm. He still had that half-smile. "I'll look for you later this evening on the deck if we haven't started firing by then."

I nodded. And firing? What does he mean? But we were being observed. We each turned and went our own way.

Making my way along the deck, I was quite sure I heard a mourning dove. But how? We were too far from land. They never fly out this far. But I needed to hurry.

I made my way back to the galley, which is where I should have been. The cleaning up was not complete. Sure enough, Cook let me have it. He reamed me up one side and down the other as to how I wouldn't amount to a hill of beans if I didn't take care.

"Now here," he said. "Take dis on down to them gentlemens staying in dat forwa'd cabin. Think they's some kind a prisoners but no one's said so far – just told to keep 'em fed."

He handed me a wood platter that held three bowls of stew with a few extra potatoes thrown in. They were getting leftovers, but it all appeared to be good enough. There was a full loaf of bread and a small crock of butter.

"Hand it through the door. And don' touch any of 'em, case they's prisoners."

"Prisoners?" I asked.

"Tisn't yours to know," he answered.

"Where's it located?" He scowled at me, but how was I to know where they were?

"Are ye daft?" he asked. "Down the ladder, head fo'ward. You'll see it."

DREAD SILENCE REPOSES...

It wasn't all that easy climbing down the ladder while balancing a tray loaded with food. However, the room was easy enough to find. It was the one with a sailor standing guard at the door. I said, "from the galley." That I guess was all he needed to hear. But really, why was there a guard? If they escaped, where would they go?

The guard who couldn't have looked more bored waved me in.

Two men were sitting at a table with a third comfortably stretched out on a bunk. His snoring was quiet and uneven. I unloaded the tray onto the table with what was to pass for a meal. For a brief moment, I thought maybe I should apologize, and mention that I hadn't prepared it. Instead, I nodded and turned to leave.

Not thinking when placing the bread on the table I'd used the hand with the bound fingers. A bit of fresh blood had soaked through the rag. The older of the two, a frown creasing his brow said "Wait a minute. Where's all that blood coming from?"

I looked down at my fingers. "Oh," I said, having given it little attention. "Careless. I was cutting up some fruit." I tried to wrap my hand in my shirttail to get it out of sight. I didn't need everyone to know of my clumsiness.

"Well, it appears you cut more than just fruit!" He picked up my hand. "You'll need to put something on that, or they'll be cutting those fingers off when they turn putrid."

My shock must surely have shown. "Keep them clean and smear a bit of honey on them, that'll keep it from festering."

Well, I thought, that's exactly what Mum would've done. For just a moment a wave of homesickness washed over me.

My eyes no doubt showed mistrust. "I suppose I should," I answered. And then wondered how he would know anything about wounds? I must have looked distrustful.

"I've seen enough accidents that lead to loss of fingers when something such as that was ignored."

I didn't really answer, just wrapped my shirttail more tightly around my hand.

"Trust me," he said as I backed away. "I'm a

doctor. I'm from just outside of Upper Marl-boro." He paused. "You'd know where that is if you were from the area." He looked at me more closely.

"Yes, I'm from the area," was my answer although I wasn't quite sure where Upper Marlboro was. Probably from the west side of our Bay. Regardless, I wasn't sure if I believed him. The doctor part that is. Why would they confine a doctor on a big ship? The other fellow sitting at the table was silent, seeming to be content spending his time observing and not commenting.

I had more than a few questions like if he was in fact a doctor, why was he imprisoned on a British ship? And if he was from this area, why were they taking him away? Impressed maybe? Is that how they staffed this entire ship? The Brits seemed to be in the minority, yet they flew the British flag.

But good sense took over. It was really none of my business and I needed to not be asking questions of things that didn't concern me.

Slipping out the door, I returned to the gal-ley. There'd be more to do, I was sure. But first I found the honey and when Cook wasn't giving it any attention dabbed a bit on the sliced fingers, then wrapped it again in one of the cleaner rags.

The chores were endless. Cook must have been feeding well over a few hundred men, the tasks seemed to never get done. They ate in shifts, so when one was done, there was a whole other group to be fed.

It appeared that my job was to feed and clean up the officer's mess and to always be at the ready should any need arise.

Gerard, the young boy was tasked with tending to the sailors in the other mess hall. There were four different seatings, so his job was never done. It felt as though as soon as one meal was cleaned up, the next was started. My job included pouring tea, keeping the cups of grog filled, and the baskets of bread and bis-cuits available. It was a lot easier than Gerard's, but he really liked what he was doing and being part of a ship's crew. He said with any luck he would someday be out of the galley and up on deck and be a real sailor.

It quickly became obvious that we would have little time off. I was fortunate – maybe be-cause I was the youngest, or not very big, or didn't seem to know what I was doing, but the officer's mess was smaller and easier to keep up with. It appeared they were better behaved as more than once Gerard complained of being smacked by one of the sailors who didn't think he was quick enough.

But now, night was on us. Stars twinkled in a cloudless sky. The shush of the water as we cut through the waves should have been a comforting sound. It was a sound I'd heard so often when I was off in a skiff when Pa would have errands on the mainland. Well, now it wasn't comforting at all. It was taking me further from home.

I had gotten a brief glimpse of the officer who had spoken to me on deck. He nodded only as he had far too much to do to engage in any conversation. It would also, no doubt, seem odd if an officer was observed chatting with a mess boy,

By tomorrow, if what I'd heard was correct, we'd be in Baltimore. Maybe there'd be a way to get off the ship. I searched the darkening shoreline; escape would be unlikely. We were too far from land or anything familiar.

The cannons were primed. The cannonballs were neatly stacked, and guns were polished and ready. I was quite sure this was not where I wanted to be.

Trying to stay in the shadows, I slipped

down the ladder and headed for my hammock. Tired as I was, the night was endless. I tossed and turned and couldn't find a comfortable way to sleep. My blanket was scratchy and the burlap I used for a pillow offered little comfort. But then I was joined by my new furry friend. Not sure why she'd picked me out of all the warm sleeping bodies. Most had far more spacious sleeping spaces than mine. But there she was. It felt good listening to her soft purring. And the warmth from her furry body felt good.

The night was quiet. There wasn't much chop to the waves, and it felt as though we were cutting through them without much effort. The masts creaked with a friendly sound with the occasional slap of a slack sail. Ropes thunked against the mast creating a soothing sound but still sleep wouldn't come.

I'm sure it was long before dawn when Cook swatted me on my rear end. I jumped. "What're ya gonna do? Sleep all the livelong day?" he asked. "And what the devil is that danged cat doing in yer hammock again. He's 'sposed to be after them rats. You best not be feedin' 'im," he said.

I wasn't feeding her, and she joined me! I didn't go find her, but I didn't need to tell him that. I threw the rag of a blanket back. She jumped down and padded off making no sound. Off to start her day's work no doubt. The freedom I thought. Would I ever have that again? She can just walk off and spend her day however she'd like. I guess I was feeling even more trapped but was sure no one would care.

"I'm coming," I murmured and yawned hugely. He didn't hear me; he was already on his way back to the galley.

Off I went, half asleep. I stood at the wood board with all its gashes and indentations from past chopping and slicing and abuse and awaited my orders.

"Here," he said, "Cut them 'tatoes and not any too small." He hefted a huge basket of brown potatoes to the board.

"You fry 'em up. I got the eggs. This'll do for today." He wiped his nose on the already soiled sleeve. "Get them biscuits baked up."

"They're not gonna be sittin' still today," he said. "More'n likely they're just gonna grab somethin' and keep movin'"

I wanted to ask why but held my tongue as I was sure I should know what he was talking about.

Frying up the potatoes with the bit of onion

that I threw in, didn't take long and was complete by the time the biscuits came out of the oven. It had taken more than two loads of wood to keep it at just the right temperature.

The bong sounded. I rushed to fill the baskets and brought them out to the tables already occupied by a few of the sleepy-eyed officers. They seemed quiet but alert with little conversation, just worried eyes looking all around. The sun wasn't up as one after another straggled in. One or two actually nodded at me. Maybe they were getting to know me.

Trying hard not to be too obvious I listened to the back and forth hesitant and brief chatter. Maybe I could learn what their plan was.

"Won't be long," said one, as he dunked his biscuit in his tea. "Ayup," said his seatmate. He was trying to dislodge the crumbs stuck in his beard and was having little luck.

"Cain't see much yet, but we gotta be gettin' close."

"Bawl-a-more here we come." Laughed another. He wasn't English. He had the sound of an American from the south. Why I wondered would he be part of the crew on a British ship? Impressed no doubt like so many others. But like Gerard, the other galley boy, maybe it offered a job with not only money but a steady supply of food. For me? All I wanted was to go home!

"Guns are all in readiness," said the one sitting opposite. He was busy wiping at the dribbles at the corners of his mouth. This one had a distinct English accent, not like the more casual speech of the Americans.

The one slurping his tea laughed, "Gonna give them Rebels a what-for with them cannons."

"'Spect we'll make it sometime today," said his buddy as he stuffed more biscuits into his mouth.

Was that I wondered the plan? It was easy enough to see we were heading up the Bay, and Baltimore wasn't that much further. I did know that much. But were they really going to use those cannons to fire on Baltimore?

My officer friend nodded to me, almost imperceptibly. Our eyes met for a moment only. I think my heart skipped a beat.

HALF CONCEALS, HALF DISCLOSES …

How long had I been on this creaking, swaying ship? It felt like forever. Not sure why, but I hadn't been seasick although a queasiness snuck up on me more than once.

I tried to stay in the shadows and keep my head down and stay out of the way hoping I'd be left alone. I did keep an eye out for my new friend with the blue eyes, the young officer who was most certainly an American. But he was not to be found.

We were on what I'd heard tell was the HMS Tonnant. It was a very large warship with many very large guns. It was frightening, to say the least.

And now, they were preparing to pull the anchor.

In an instant, the whole ship suddenly came alive. Sails were unfurled. Orders were given.

Everyone was on some mission. The sailors were running back and forth all giving attention to what they were tasked with. Many were busy stacking even more of the heavy black balls next to the huge cannons. It all had a menacing and foreboding look.

I was trying to look busy sweeping the deck so's I'd be left to myself and not assigned to any-thing. I was also trying to determine if there was any possible way that I could disappear over the side. Maybe even if I could toss a piece of scrap lumber into the water. Maybe hang on-to it 'til I'd drift ashore. There had to be a way to escape. Disappear before their war started.

Then not quite sure what happened or why, but a sailor, who appeared too ancient to be off to sea grabbed my arm with his grimy hand. "Dis way." That's all he said.

His eye patch wasn't doing a very good job of hiding an empty eye socket. It wiggled and the tie threatened to come undone with each step. He dragged me to the side of the ship. Was he throwing me overboard? I shrank back but watched as two sailors were busy adjusting a ragged-looking rope ladder that hung over the side. A much smaller boat was tied up below. It was rocking gently in the waves.

"Dis'll keep ya out of da way," he said. I didn't move. "They wants you off the ship, dang it. Move," he said. "Git on down there. Now."

Looking over the side I wasn't sure what I was supposed to do. It was a long way down and too far to jump.

He saw the hesitation. "Da ladder," he said looking at me with his one eye as if asking was I some sort of fool. "Git yer'self down there, and do it now." And as he said it, another sailor scrambled down the side. He looked like a long-legged spider gingerly stepping from one stretch of rope to the other.

I wasn't sure if I could do this but the push from the one-eyed sailor convinced me that was what I was going to do, like it or not.

With caution, I swung one leg over the side, trying to look like I knew just what I was about. I moved one foot at a time down the side. I'd never been on a rope ladder before, and it was truly wobbly. The thought of falling was frightening. I held on tight. I caught a quick glimpse of the three men below who weren't in uniform. They were the same who had been confined to the cabin where I had delivered dinner - the prisoners who weren't really prisoners! And of course, that was when I made a misstep. I couldn't catch myself and tumbled the last few feet, landing with a thud on the deck. I'd missed the bottom rung of the rope ladder.

The old Doc was standing over me. Concern etched around tired eyes. He bent to help me up. The nice-looking younger gentlemen offered a hand too.

"There now young fella'" he said, "You don't want to be sprawled on the deck when this all begins."

I must have had a confused look.

"I believe they've separated us from the ship so's we hear nothing. I also suspect there's some bargaining that could go on, should they want to release us. Best to keep us separate."

"But...," I started.

He answered before I could get it out. "you're probably here as a deckhand and cook to tend to whatever we should need."

I had so many more questions like when "this all begins"? What did that mean? But I kept still. A sharp pain started to creep across my shoulder. I wanted to cry out. Blood was seeping through my shirt.

The Doc saw it. "Here," he said, "Let's take care of that." He didn't wait for an answer but took me by the arm and walked me over to the side of the boat.

"We've got a bucket of water here," he said. "It'll take but a moment to get you cleaned up." He started to pull down the top of my shirt. We had a struggle as to whether or not he was going to pull it off.

"Here now," he said, "this isn't going to hurt." His voice was sympathetic but firm. He yanked back the collar pulling it down to expose the gash. He gasped.

"Oh my," he said. His face turned red. His raised eyebrows asked a question. I looked down choosing not to acknowledge what he had discovered.

His voice was low. "I'm sorry," he said, "I had no idea. I didn't know girls were allowed on ships." There was half a smile as he tried to adjust my top. "Here," he said, "Let me help you."

"I'm sorry," he said. "I didn't know." He rolled up my sleeve trying to get to the wound. "But it's all right," he said. "You already know I'm a doctor. Name's Doc Beanes. And aren't you the one with the cut fingers?"

I held up my hand with the two thin pieces of rag tied around the fingertips.

"I'm fine," I said.

"Well now," he said, "We'll take a look at

those too, while we're at it." He began swabbing at the wound near my shoulder. The rag he used was instantly bloodied. "It'll be fine," he said. "Doesn't appear to be very deep. Just lots of blood."

I hardly dared speak but, in a whisper, asked why he was on this boat and why they had moved us down here.

"Well now," he said, "I'm what you might call a captive. That would maybe be someone who's not quite a prisoner." He smiled. 'The Brits have been having their fair share of problems with me, but now they just want to keep me out of harm's way." He cleared his throat and continued in a low voice meant only for my ears.

"I was a prisoner of the Brits, but they're now realizing I'd been more of a help than a hindrance to them. I'd patched up many of their soldiers while they were on their foray through our area. I don't think they were aware of all the aid I had rendered." And then as an afterthought added, "Regardless of their loyalties."

He gave me a half-smile. "There'd been some serious fighting with many wounded. I'm a doctor." He shrugged. "Which side they'd been fighting on was of no concern to me. They needed patching up and that's what I seem to do best."

He was busy tying the bandage tightly around my wounded arm and shoulder. "I'd patched up a number of them and then they threw me in the brig."

He sort of snickered. "I wasn't doing anyone much good locked up, but then my friend Key over there showed up. Nice fellow. Old friend and he's a lawyer who seems to know what he's about. Then they brought in Skinner to negotiate my release." He was smiling. "He's the gentleman over there," he said pointing to a fellow reclining against the mast.

"Didn't know I was worth all this attention but then they decided maybe it would be best to allow the negotiation of my release." He lowered his voice. "So now," he said, "I'm sort of free. However, their concern is that we all know far too much of their battle plans and they've decided not to grant us our freedom until all this is over."

"Until all what is over?" I asked.

"Unfortunately," he answered, "or maybe fortunately I don't know all the details that they think I know, but we'll all know soon enough. There's going to be trouble one way or another."

"Francis," he called over to his friend, "Come

over and meet my latest patient." He ripped the long end of the rag and tied it securely. "Tell me your name young miss," he said and instantly corrected himself, ... "young sir." I cringed hoping no one had heard his slip.

"My name is Mackenzie," I said. His companion put out his hand – "How do you do," he said. "My name is Francis Scott Key, and I'm an old friend of the good doctor here, Doc Beanes."

"He's actually my lawyer who has been kind enough to spend some time trying to negotiate my release. And that's my other friend Mr. Skinner over there." He cleared his throat, "Now of course, whether I've been released or not, it appears we're going to be in for a bit of trouble."

"Indeed we are," agreed Mr. Key. "If memory serves me right, we're about to pull into the port of Baltimore. And" he said looking out over the vast expanse of water, "With all these ships it can't be good. There's going to be trouble. I'm only hoping we can get back on dry land before all Hell breaks loose." His brows were knit together. "Pardon my language," he added.

"We three are captives," said Mr. Key, "Although they're not calling us that. But with luck, we'll get back on dry land shortly."

"But," said the Doctor eyeing me with curiosity, "tell me why you are on this British ship. Girls do not belong on ships," he said. His voice was low. Key heard him and his raised eyebrows showed his surprise.

And why not, girls on ships, I wanted to ask. But before the words would come out, he answered the question, "It's bad luck."

Mr. Key was eyeing me, holding back his amusement. "Well do tell Doc Beanes," he said. "He's such a nice-looking young fellow, now isn't he Doctor." His eyes scrunched up in a smile.

"I was kidnaped," I answered, my voice low. "My home is on Poplar Island. They came not long ago and grabbed me. I was home alone and tending to our farm."

For a moment I thought tears would start to fall. I bit my lip trying to stay calm. They began to ask lots of questions. We continued in hushed voices. Only the three of us could hear.

"Those Brits," I said, "they've pillaged our island so often it's a wonder anything is left." Now a tear did fall. "I've heard tell that they've taken many of the Islander's chickens and sheep and even a cow. There's little left for us to get through the winter months."

"There's a war on," said Key. "Nothing is

safe."

"Our home was safe until a few days ago." I said, not intending to be quarrelsome. "We live out on the end of the island and we're aways from where they came ashore."

The good doctor patted me on the back. "You'll be fine," he said. "This has to end eventually. Somehow, we'll all get out of this. "But" he added, "I think we're going to be in for a time before it's all over."

"Well," said the fellow named Key, "They're not going to release us 'til they're done with whatever they have planned for Baltimore." He looked out toward the horizon and shook his head. "It might be a while," he added.

"They've agreed to release us but they're not going to do it just yet," he added. His voice was low. "They're going to wait 'til they sack the city. I guess we all know too much, and their concern is that we'll tip off the militia."

"And that we would," whispered the Doctor, "If we could get away from this danged ship." He rolled my sleeve back down. He was finished dressing my wound.

THE LAND OF THE FREE
AND THE HOME OF THE BRAVE...

We were confined to a small boat. It was tied to the HMS Tonnant, which could only be described as a warship. Canons were poking through the sides, the blackness ominous of what was to come.

What was I supposed to do? How could I escape? Where would I go?

We were being observed by what looked like a naval officer on the ship that was towering over us. It was frightening. We were being towed. Towed by a warship into what was to come.

But it was him! Staring down at us, was the midshipman with the deep blue eyes. He was watching us closely from the deck high above us. He couldn't have heard our conversation, but his look was one of concern. He turned and we could hear his voice, raised with authority, giving instructions.

"Go on below decks," said Doc Beanes, and in the same breath, "Weren't you the kitchen help on the big ship?"

I nodded. "Then that's no doubt why they've sent you onto this boat. They could no doubt use your help in the galley." He lowered his voice, "We three are prisoners of sorts. You need to stay out of the way should anything get started."

Prisoners I thought. What if they started firing at them or decided to throw them overboard?

But he was of course correct, I was there as the galley help and if nothing else, it would keep me out of the way of any trouble. Whatever fate was planned for the "prisoners", it would no doubt be best to keep out of sight.

We had been tied up to the Tonnant, which I was to learn, was a British naval warship. It had more cannons than I could count. This wasn't good I was sure, and now we were being towed in a small sloop – to keep us out of the way? Well, that was Doc Beanes belief and only a handful of us were on board. A couple of disinterested sailors were going to and fro, checking the lines and not in any great rush to do much else. We were being towed after all, so there was little for them to do. The sails hadn't even been hoisted.

I ducked into the hatchway, using the smoothed rails to slide down to the lower deck. Following my nose, I easily found the galley. The pleasant smell of a meal being prepared wafted through the air. Above, I could hear shouts going back and forth between the Tonnant and our small vessel. It was frightening. Especially to be below decks and not know what was next.

But I slipped through the door and moved with silent footsteps, over to the chopping block. Although it was a much smaller galley than what had been on the bigger ship it was much tidier.

Picking up the knife I began to slice the warm bread. It was fresh from the oven. I ignored the cook who was busy with a huge kettle of soup, bubbling away sending fragrant clouds of good smells into the air.

He didn't notice me immediately as he was busy stirring the steaming pot. I ignored him. The scent of the fresh-made stew reminded me how hungry I was. I quick snuck a piece of bread before he'd notice.

"Ah now," he said, "this won't last long."

And oh my gosh! It was Gerard. How had he gotten into this position? "They're going to gobble this up. Smell. It's wonderful is it not?"

He looked over at me. "Ahhh," he said. "It be you. Huh, wonder why'd they send both of us?" He gave what may have been a smile. "Wonder what Cook's gonna do with two of us gone?" He laughed. "Best we get goin' on this or we both gonna be sent back. Lots easier on a small ship."

"Well, they said you'd be needing an assistant. Said I had experience so was sent to help." I smiled and picked up the knife, "Give me a moment and I'll have all this bread in baskets and out on the table." I think he was pleased that it was me.

"And is it oyster stew, that you're cooking up?" I asked. It wasn't hard to recognize the scent that so often wafted up from Mum's stove. It brought waves of homesickness.

And he wasn't cooking it properly! I suspected he'd been boiling it for hours in what looked like a very thin broth. It just wasn't going to create a very good meal.

"Yup," he answered, "It be stew. "Hadn't made it before. Givin' it a try. Found a pile of them oysters stashed in a corner. Musta gotten 'em off the Island."

My island I wanted to say, and they probably stole them as they undoubtedly didn't know
anything about oyster tonging either, our meth-
od of capturing lots of tasty oysters.

He continued stirring. He was wearing the
cook's hat that was much too big and was
threatening to fall off. It sat at an angle nearly
covering one eye. "Ya think more potatoes maybe?" He was staring into the pot. He winced as
he tasted the burning liquid. "Here, give it a try."
He was holding the wooden spoon offering a
taste.

The boat lurched nearly knocking me off my
feet. We both had to reach out to the table to
steady ourselves. The knife was sharp, and I
came close to slicing my fingers - again.

"It's good," I said.

And then, it seemed like minutes only, we
heard the benches sliding back as the crewmen
took their places at the table. I brought out the
baskets of bread hoping to stall them a bit while
Gerard finished up the stew. I filled their mugs
with the grog. They were enjoying themselves
sparing back and forth so paid little heed to the
delayed stew.

They had been enjoying their time and had

given scant attention to us. One laughed at me – "He's a slip of a thing now ain't he," he joked. "Hey boy, where's the butter, and we're gonna need more bread over here to go with it." Then they laughed as if someone had told a great joke. I grabbed the empty basket as he reached out and gave me a pinch on my derriere. They laughed uproariously. I moved quickly to get out of reach.

I pulled my cap lower. My hair kept escaping. It did not want to be pulled back and tied. There wasn't really enough of it to do anything but tuck it into my cap. There was enough dirt on my face I was sure, so's it was hard to tell just who I was. I tried to swagger and take long strides much like what boys seem to do.

Sweat beaded up and I swiped at it with my sleeve as I moved back and forth trying to tend to everything at once. There were only four sailors so not that much to do other than stay out of arm's reach.

They lost interest in taunting me and instead spoke among themselves. I kept my head low and gave attention only to serving and cleaning up spills while picking up some of the chatter that went back and forth. I did not want them to know I was listening to their every word.

The discussion was a bit shocking, and I tried to not look interested as I continued to fill the breadbasket and the empty bowls. But as I brought in even more of the overcooked stew, the conversation got more disturbing.

"Sacked Washington awright didn't we," which was followed by laughter. They were Brits – all of them, with accents that were sometimes difficult to understand.

"Got 'em good. Indeed, even sacked that President's house. Ha, did ya see them flames? That'll teach them danged upstarts."

"On to Ball-a-moh," said the one with the scraggly beard. Breadcrumbs clung to the tangles of the greying hair.

"We'll fix 'em," said his companion. "Should be easy enough. Heard tell they don' know we be on our way. Ha!" he added. "We'll show them rebel Americans a thing or two." Laughter followed.

Was it true? Did Baltimore not know they were on their way? I wondered. And in fact, if that was the destination, was there no way to get word to them?

And, it truly did sound like Washington had been sacked. Could it really be? Maybe burned to the ground. There were too many questions, but I had to bring food up to the deck to the three who were called prisoners. It appeared that they were getting no attention at all. It took two trips to bring up enough for all and I truly wanted to chat with them and share what I'd heard but it was near impossible with only two of us tending the galley.

The meal was over, and I was worn. The crew had returned to the deck, probably as look-outs and to watch the prisoners. Watch them for what I thought. There was nowhere that they could go!

Gerard was finishing up and seemed pleased that I'd been there. At least he said nothing about doing anything wrong. After I'd washed the last bowl and rinsed the mop, he shooed me off with "G'wan get outta here." Was he being nice to me? And why? But he didn't have to say it twice. I was out the door.

It took moments only to get back up on deck for air. Below deck was often fetid with the close quarters with everything always seeming a bit damp. And now, maybe I'd find a moment to have a word with the prisoners. I wanted to tell them the little I knew of the plan that I'd heard.

But now, the big ship had dropped anchor. Mr. Key and Doc Beanes were busy watching the men slipping off the Tonnant and into the longboats.

He knew! Probably knew a lot more than I did. He saw me watching. "Headed for land no doubt," he said. "They're heavily armed so no telling what's going to take place." His voice was just above a whisper.

"We're being further detained," said the Doctor. He had deep worry lines etched between his eyebrows. When he saw the confused look on my face he added, "They had said they were going to let us off in Baltimore, but now I'm not so sure. There's no telling how they're going to move us if their plan is to invade the city." I was quite sure he wasn't telling me everything. He knew far more than what I had heard.

"Hmmmm," said Mr. Key. "I do know that that's North Point, over there." He was pointing to the land that wasn't all that far off. "It appears that that's where they're all landing. That's not Baltimore," he added. "Baltimore has a fort," he added, "but it's still aways away."

And sure enough, they hadn't been on land but a short time when we heard shots fired. It was frightening.

There were other very large ships in the area. All flying the British flag. The sun was doing its best to break through the low grey clouds. We watched in silence as more and more soldiers came down the rope ladders into the waiting boats. It could have been chaotic, but they moved in near silence, each with a weapon slung over his shoulder, each focused on his mission.

There were so many ships it was hard to determine just how many were surrounding us. Anchors held them in place. Most had sails pulled and tied securely to the yardarms.

We stood at the rail, mesmerized by what was transpiring. The shots were endless. We winced as distant screams traveled over the water. How were we ever going to get free of this? And, when they finished here, were we going to be shipped to England? What about my family? How would they know?

And then there was that call of the mourning dove. I was sure I heard it. It was from high up in the rigging of the Tonnant. Did I really hear that? Doves are usually land birds. That was odd. I strained to look but could see nothing.

The shots continued to ring out. Would they be firing at us next?

THE HAVOC OF WAR...

The soldiers continued scrambling down the sides of the ships and then rowing with all due haste to the land. I stood, squinting into the distance, trying to think of some way that I could get ashore. But the sounds and smoke rising in the air, and the noise rolling across the water from the battle was frightening. Even if I could get ashore what would I do? Where would I go? How could I stay hidden 'til the battle was over?

The three men who were not in uniform, who were prisoners, were silent. Their brows were furrowed and now and again one would try to say a word to the other as they watched the smoke rise from the shore. Gunshots echoed through the air. The sounds were terrifying. I moved closer to the group standing at the rail. I began to ask questions.

Doc Beanes was the closest so I wouldn't have to raise my voice to be heard. He was also the easiest to chat with. Between the gunfire and orders being yelled on the Tonnant, we were able to chat. He told me a bit more about the three, although he seemed a mite hesitant. He said Mr. Key had lived in Baltimore and was now a lawyer in Georgetown, just outside of Washington. He had been sent to secure his release. The Doc said he was being held prisoner by the Brits on suspicion of aiding the enemy. And who was the enemy? That would be us – the Americans, he said.

He went on to say it was all a trumped-up charge as he'd done more than anyone to patch up and try to repair the wounds of the British militia. Nevertheless, they weren't about to let him go. He said that fellow over there who was named Skinner, which I already knew, but he added, he's also an American. Doc Beanes said his purpose was to negotiate his release. The Doc said he'd been successful. Well, if all three were now confined to this ship I wasn't sure how successful he'd been in getting them released!

The fighting and gunshots continued as he told me a bit more about Washington D.C. To hear him tell it, there was nothing left of the city!

"But" he admitted, "I hadn't been there and had only heard tell."

Well, I'd never been there but Pa had when he was younger. He said it was as muddy as all get out, but it seemed to always be bustling with activity. Everyone there he said was busy, rushing from here to there. All seemed to be on a mission.

I'd seen drawings in our schoolbook of the White House and the Capitol building where most of our laws are made. My secret hope was to someday get there. Mr. Key had been listening intently and added that when he left the city much of it was on fire, including both the White House and the Capitol building.

"And then," added Key, "the next day I was negotiating the release of Beanes here." He smiled and pointed to the good doctor. "And then," he paused maybe for emphasis, "as if we hadn't had enough, a huge storm came in." He rubbed at the crease in his forehead. "There was a tornado. I saw it, even from the distance where we were standing."

His look was more of bafflement than anything else. "It apparently touched down in the city and there was even more damage! The rains did put out most of the fires. Or so I was told," he added. So, that no doubt was the same storm that had traveled across to our island!

Key was a nice fellow, and he wasn't finished. "However, they wanted us out of there and so escorted us to the fleet of ships in the Potomac River. And here we are."

The relief that both showed was remarkable.

"It was a close call. We weren't sure if they wanted to execute us or use us for a prisoner exchange, or," he added, "if the plan was to ship us off to a jail in England."

"We're fortunate," the Doc said, "They haven't been as good to others. But then Mr. Key here knows what he's about. Don't you now Francis?" There was a knowing smile that passed between them.

"Tell me now," said Key, "And I'm not sure how you want to answer this or even if you can answer, but there's talk that you're an American spy who was deliberately captured."

My first instinct was to laugh. Do they really think I'd be in this position if I was a spy? Goodness me, I thought. A spy for who? I lived on a small island of fewer than 100 people. We had little to do with this war. Well anyway until they decided to land on our shores.

I must have looked baffled, but he continued. "The good Doctor told me about the confusion as to who you are." He had lowered his voice even more. "I'm aware that you're a young lady." He harrumphed a bit and then said, "Of course, your secret is safe with us."

Did they really think I'd allow myself to be kidnapped and then dress as a boy to become a spy? I must have stammered the answer. "No indeed," I said. "I'm not a spy. I'm a farm girl. I live on Poplar Island. Would I ever knowingly let myself get into this predicament?" Tears began welling up. "I want to go home." I didn't mean to sound quite so much like a baby but there it was. A lone tear slid down my cheek.

"You'll be home soon enough child. I'm sure of it." Mr. Key was patting my hand. "We've already negotiated Doc Beanes release," he said and then added, "if we can ever get off this ship. We'll see if we can have you released too, maybe as part of his staff. Maybe as his "boy" or caretaker."

"Regardless," said Beanes, "There's going to be trouble for sure. And" he added, "they're not ready, and they're going to need more help than I can give them."

I swiped at another tear not wanting them to see. How would I ever get back to my island?

OUR FLAG WAS STILL THERE...

The hours dragged on. There was little conversation as we watched to see what was next. The Tonnant, with our small sloop firmly tied to their stern, had been anchored here for what felt like days - but had only been hours. Mr. Key had said it was North Port where the troops were landing. It was not Baltimore.

The shooting was endless. The sounds reverberated through the air. I wanted to cover my ears. Smoke rose in puffs and the sound of screams seemed to bounce off the waves. And then there they were, the small boats returning to the ships. Rowers feverishly digging their oars deep into the water. They carried what looked like more than a few wounded.

There had to have been hundreds of soldiers who had left for the shore. We had watched in awe as they just kept scrambling down the sides of all the ships into the boats below. But now, we watched in near disbelief as the boats were being rowed with all due haste, back to the ships.

The oarsmen pulled hard at the oars propelling the boats through the choppy water. It wasn't looking good for the Brits. Each dory held wounded. They looked beaten and defeated, their faces drawn. Some with obvious wounds, blood splattering their uniforms. Others slumped over. We could hear the moans even from this distance.

We watched. Words wouldn't come. We could do nothing. We were confined to the sloop. The sloop that was tied to the Tonnant. And we were being observed closely by the seamen on our boat. The Doc's two friends, Mr. Key and Mr. Skinner must have been very important as the crew on our small sloop kept a close eye on them. Fearing an escape maybe? But where or how they could have gotten away was a mystery. I too kept a close eye. If they were going over the side, so was I!

Doc Beanes was soon pressed into service with all the returning injured. A sailor who had been watching us from the deck of the Tonnant climbed down the rope ladder to our small craft. He went directly to the Doc and ordered him to, "Come with me."

Together they scrambled up the rope ladder,

Doc Beanes not quite as confident as the limber sailor. Too much was happening. Boats going back and forth to the shore, men scrambling up and down the rope ladders. Noise and confusion everywhere.

It appeared that the returning men had very bad wounds or at least it seemed that way with all the blood. Doc Beanes surely was going to have his hands full.

The day dragged on, the screaming, the orders being given and everyone in a rush either scrambling up the rope ladders or scrambling back down to the small boats. By nightfall, it appeared that most had returned to the anchored ships. And then, quite unexpectedly, the Tonnant pulled its anchor and raised its sails. They turned in the direction of the harbor.

Baltimore Harbor said Mr. Key.

We remained in the open air on the deck, having no idea what was next. Sleep wouldn't come. The night dragged on. We heard the call of every gull and the splash of every wakeful fish. It was a long night.

And then just after the first rays of sun poked over the horizon - the firing started again, only now it was the boom of the deep bellied cannons.

It was dreadful. It was sudden. It was deafening. It was frightening. It didn't stop. The Tonnant had dropped anchor with our small sloop still tied aft of the big ship.

It was so confusing. The noise, the bedlam.

Mr. Key said we were now in the Baltimore Harbor. There were booms. There were bombs bursting in the air. The noise, the confusion, the sailors yelling. Orders being given. It was a complete and frightening bedlam.

Had there been a plan? More of a plan than all the fighting at North Point?

We had no knowledge of what was to happen next. We weren't even certain if this had been the Brits intended destination! Mr. Key and his friend Mr. Skinner said they were quite sure that's why they were still being held. The Brits thought that the two may have known of the plan. The plan to invade Baltimore. Both said they knew nothing of any plans to invade anywhere.

And the canons! I have never heard the like. It was frightening. The British ships were firing one after another into the air with huge earsplitting blasts. Most burst in the air. It was hard to see if any were landing on the Baltimore fort. It was Fort McHenry said Mr. Key and that was their target.

I held my hands over my ears, but it didn't help. It sounded like the worst most violent thunderstorm that had ever come off the Bay. The air around us vibrated with each boom. Each flash lit up the night sky.

The sounds! So loud! We had no idea who was in trouble and if anyone would be able to claim victory. And then the thought that we may never get off this sloop. We could be sunk if we were hit by any of the cannons firing from the shore.

How could we be rescued by the Americans? Did they even know we were here? And a frightening thought: If we weren't rescued, we no doubt would be considered prisoners. Would we then be sent off to England? To prison?

Key said something about courage to me and then said we were in an American truce ship, that's why we'd been removed from the Tonnant and onto this small sloop. But did all those military people firing the cannons know that?

The Americans, in what Key said was Ft. McHenry, were firing back with their cannons. There were so many explosions, and the cannonballs were dropping everywhere. It was hard to breathe, the air thick with smoke. It was truly hard to tell if any of the shots hit their mark. And then the ships began to move back. Away from the Fort.

"Out of range," said Key by way of explanation. The chaos just continued.

Then the rain started. We stood at the side of our small sloop and were almost instantly drenched. The noise. The screaming of the bombs and cannon was frightening. There was no way to block out the racket and chaos. And the rain poured down, down through the blinding, thick smoke. There were screams that cut like a knife through the air. For a moment only, I wondered if I'd be better off jumping over the side and swimming to shore.

It truly sounded like the end of the world. It was well into the night. The hours ticked by. For a brief time, I tried to curl up on a corner of the deck with a scrap of blanket. I tried to sleep. But the blasts that were shrieking through the air, would give no peace. There wasn't a way to describe it. It was frightening.

And then I was up. Sleep would not come. The sky was lightening on the eastern horizon. Both the fellow named Skinner and Mr. Key had never left the side of our sloop but had stood all night watching the bombardment in horror.

And then the rain stopped, just like that after a full night of endless, mostly pouring rain. It ended.

So did the blasts from the cannons and the explosions!

We were too far out in the harbor to have been hit or even targeted said Mr. Key, but still – the noise, the screams, the smoke, the rain, and the fright from seeing all those bursting shells. It had been terrifying.

The Brits ceased their firing. The noise stopped. The sudden silence had us all looking about in disbelief.

And then, the sky began to lighten. And there it was.

A huge, enormous, almost indescribable massive flag!

It was flying with such grandeur over the Fort.

At first, it was difficult to see in the early morning light. There was smoke and haze from all the cannon fire. But then, the light from the sun began to burn through the thinning haze. Slowly it became clear.

It was our flag.

And the size! I had never seen the like. The smoke and fog were clearing. For a moment there was near silence. We stared at the red and white stripes and the 15 white stars on the blue background. The flag blew nearly straight out in the wind. We stood, astonished. No words would come. It was our flag.

Everything stopped.

It appeared that even the Brits for a moment came to attention. And then, even from this distance, we were sure we could hear a flute playing "Yankee Doodle".

Key was in awe as the scene unfolded in front of us. He began to take notes on the back of an envelope. It was a sight to be seen and he was going to record it.

The world was at attention. Everything had stopped. A lone gull flew over, gliding in the wind. His screech broke the spell. It brought us back to where we were.

"Wait for us here," said Key. The two speaking in low voices disappeared below deck. They needed to gather their belongings. They were sure during this pause that it wouldn't be long before they would be released. Maybe they would be delivered to the shore.

TWILIGHT'S LAST GLEAMING ...

A sailor, his voice filled with anger, yelled from the deck high above us to "Make haste and get on up here 'fore we have ye flogged for desertion."

He was speaking to me!

Well, I wasn't exactly sure how I could be accused of desertion when I wasn't in their British Navy. Good sense took over. Best to pay heed or there'd be trouble for sure.

"Git on up here and don' be givin' me any trouble," said the nearly toothless sailor. His speech was slurred with the missing teeth, and his hair hung in tangles drooping in his eyes. I wondered how he could even see.

"Git on up dis ladder," he said, yanking on the ladder. It hung like a limp rag over the side. "Git on now."

He didn't have to tell me twice. I didn't want to know the consequences if I didn't follow his orders. Going up, I was a lot more limber than earlier when I had fallen in a heap coming down - when I'd landed at the feet of Doc Beanes.

Scrambling from one step to another my bare feet felt the scratchiness of the rope. I jumped over the side onto the deck. And just like that. I was back on the ship. This was not where I wanted to be. And then there was Gerard, scrambling up behind me. He leaped over the side and without even a nod, made haste to the galley.

"You too," he said. "Git on down there." He was toothless and spittle flew through the air with each word.

"But" I stammered. "I'm going with them." I pointed to the sloop below.

"Yer not goin' anywheres," he said, "'cept down there." He was pointing to the hatchway to the galley.

Tears were threatening. That was when I saw Doc Beanes. He threw a leg over the side ready for his descent on the wobbling ladder. Back to the sloop.

His jacket was in disarray. There were splatters of blood on his sleeves. His eyes were tired and then he looked over and saw me. He seemed shocked to see me back on board. It was hard to tell but he may have mouthed the words, "Aren't you coming?"

Another sailor gave him a shove nearly pushing him over the side. He grasped the ladder with both hands and down he went, down the rope rungs, onto the deck of the sloop. He kept an eye on me as he descended but I was being pushed by the toothless sailor towards the hatchway.

Suddenly there was bedlam. Orders were being given: "Now hear this!"

"Raise the sails!"

"Anchor detail!"

There was more that I couldn't hear.

The anchor was ever so slowly pulled back on board. The sails were already flapping in their attempt to catch the wind. Seamen were busy completing one task after another. Everyone had a job.

I caught a glimpse as two seamen released the rope that was tying the sloop to the Tonnant. It was thrown down to the sailor below. He caught it and began to coil it on the deck, nearly at the feet of the Doctor. Our sails filled with the gusty breeze. We were pulling away.

"Oh no," I said. "I need to go with them. I shouldn't be here." Tears were blinding me.

The toothless sailor poked me in the ribs. "Yer not goin' anywheres 'cept down that ladder, now git on down der," he said pointing to the hatchway. He gave me a shove. I could see the sloop, its sails raised, already sailing off into the distance. The three were on the deck. I was sure they couldn't see me and there wasn't a way to get back down to them. I wanted to cry. Now, what would I do? I thought for a moment to jump overboard but would they shoot me? Tears threatened to spill over.

And then I heard that bird call. The call of a mourning dove. It came from high up in the rigging. Could it have been a bird? I tried to get my wits about me. That wasn't typical of a mourning dove. They tended to stay on the ground walking back and forth, making their quiet calling with their gentle cooing. I looked up, squinting high up in the sails.

I could see little. And just like that. There was a sudden gust of wind. The boat nearly danced in the breeze. We were headed out of the harbor and into the Bay. How had this happened? How would I get away? How could I get back to the sloop?

We were in the lead. There were others in the flotilla but for whatever reason they didn't seem to be in such a hurry. Maybe waiting for the troops who had been fighting on the mainland? I didn't know.

An officer yelled at the toothless sailor who had been ordering me about.

"Get that ladder up," he yelled. "We're underway."

It was my blue-eyed Midshipman. He nodded to me, but caution was necessary. I wanted to somehow get his attention to my plight. There was no way, but the toothless one had left to take up the ladder.

The cloud cover was returning, maybe from the rain that had so recently ceased or maybe from all the explosions from the cannons that had been fired through the night.

We were on our way. I tried to make sense of what was happening. The Midshipman stayed close but was busy giving orders. There was so much going on. Now was my chance. I was sure I wouldn't be noticed and started a walk around the deck, trying to look like I was on some sort of errand or mission. How could I pick up a loose board and throw it over and jump myself? There had to be some way off this ship. But how to not be noticed. Tears wanted to start.

I tried to get a glimpse of the sloop that was no doubt heading for Baltimore, but it had disappeared - and so had any chance of my ever getting away. Tears threatened to spill over.

And then the Midshipman was there. He tipped his hat, as he would for a lady, and then instantly realized what he'd done. I swiped at the tears and came close to nodding in acknowledgment. We weren't being observed but I picked up some roping and made myself busy winding it into a neat pile, trying to bring some semblance of order to the tangled heap. He continued his walk giving an order here and there while keeping an eye out that all was well. I had nearly finished winding the rope into a neat stack when he approached me again.

"You're back," he said. His voice was low and there was enough going on that we were disregarded.

"Yes, they put me back on this ship. I'm not sure why." I bit back tears that were threatening to fall.

"Well, I can tell you why," he said as his eyes bored into me. "They released the prisoner."

"What prisoner," I asked, unsure if we were talking about the same person.

"Why Beanes, of course."

"Ahh," I said, "I didn't know he was really a prisoner."

"Well actually just being held."

"And were they holding Mr. Key also?"

"Look," he said, almost apologetically, 'This is what happened, and I'm not a Brit. I'm from Boston and I was impressed into their Navy. You do know what impressed means don't you?" He was eyeing me as if I was the village idiot. But for a moment only, a finger reached out and touched my arm.

"Oh course," I answered and really didn't want to get too into it but said "My Pa had been impressed."

"Well then, you know I'm not here by choice, but chances of escaping haven't been good. They want me to be an officer in their navy." His eyes searched the horizon with a sadness that was hard to miss.

He turned his attention back to me. "But here's what's happened with Doc Beanes. Key is a lawyer from Baltimore, which you may know, and he and that other fellow negotiated his release. They thought Beanes was mistreating the Brits when he was actually trying to help any that had been wounded."

I knew that part of the story.

He cleared his throat. "Then once they had him on board, they thought he and Key knew too much of what the battle strategy would be so they couldn't release them."

"They all knew that's why they were being held," I answered. "But I need to leave too." I hoped it didn't sound like a whine. "I have no idea how to get back home."

"Are you from one of the islands on the east side of the Bay?"

"Indeed, I am," I answered. "Poplar Island."

"Well, they did grab a few unlikely people on the way up the Bay."

"Really," I said and didn't mean to have so much sass. But I went from a near crying fit to now trying to reasonably discuss how exactly I was going to get out of this mess. "How many others are there from my island?"

"Well," he answered, "I think only a boy from your area. They were more interested in procuring food."

"What boy?" I asked.

"Well, he was a little negro kid with a slouchy hat. He's everywhere but now probably down in the hold bringing up more cannonballs for our next encounter."

This wasn't good. "What next encounter?" I wanted to ask, but more importantly, what was the name of the young boy he was speaking of? My heart nearly stopped beating – could it possibly be where the call of the mourning dove had come from. I'm sure I looked confused.

I was sure he was going to say something about heading into more trouble, but then a ruckus started near the wheel of the ship. And off he went. It sounded like a rope had snapped. One of the sailors was howling. I was sure it wasn't good, but I didn't want to be a part of it.

The toothless sailor was back. He gave me a push. "What'd ya think yer doin'," he asked. "Git on outa here." His eyes were mean. I scrambled over to the hatchway and slipped down the ladder to the galley.

MISTS OF THE DEEP ...

The dinner went smoothly. There was little chatter and Cook had used a soup that he may have made a few days ago. I wasn't sure. Didn't look very tempting.

I didn't want to be stuck in the galley any longer. I know Cook was glad I was back along with Gerard, but he had nothing to say. When he got busy cleaning up the mess, I slipped out. I no longer cared what he thought.

Standing at the rail, I could see it. I was sure. It was a distance away, but it was our island. The sun was setting behind us and as far away as it was, I was sure it was my island hovering on the horizon.

I picked up a mop and tried to look as though I was busy with a chore. There were sailors everywhere. Everyone working at some task or other. They gave me little attention.

And then there was the Midshipman standing at my side.

"Mac," he said, his voice just above a whisper. "What will you do? We're sailing south. There's going to be another battle. How can I help you?" For a moment only his finger touched my arm.

"That's my home," I said, nodding towards the island that appeared larger, the further south we sailed.

I looked at him for a moment, admiring this tall stranger. "I don't even know your name," I said.

"It's Alex. Alex Winslow."

The winds were calming. The sails brushed against the yardarms. The sound somehow comforting.

"Well," I said, and my cheeks felt hot - I'm not sure why. "I need to get home. My family will have no idea what's happened to me. They're going to be so upset."

"I'd like to go with you," he answered, his voice was low, meant only for my ears. "You know I'm from Boston. I was captured three years ago. I'm 19 now and my family has no idea what's happened to me either. I've had no way to contact them."

"Impressment," I said. "I'm so sorry."

"We may be sailing further south than we've

been before," he said. "I'm quite sure I shouldn't know that but had overheard a conversation at the captain's table."

"But what can we do?" I asked.

"You may not want to come with us. I'm not sure of our destination," he answered. For a moment his fingers reached out and touched my elbow. Warmth crept all the way down to my fingertips.

"I would escape with you, but we'll both be shot if we're caught. It would be desertion."

"Maybe that boy from your island?" he said out of the blue.

"What boy?" I asked.

"You know, the one I mentioned earlier. He calls himself Rip."

"Oh my," was about all I could say.

"He's young, but he was bragging about his swimming skills," he said. "And you are also a swimmer are you not?"

I nodded, knowing I wasn't a very good swimmer. I'd gotten in the water any number of times along our shore when Mum wasn't watching. It was rare though. And when I did get off to the shore it was with the twins. Trouble was that those twins had to be watched closely. They had little understanding of what can happen in the water. Girls weren't supposed to swim but it was a good thing I could 'cause whether my parents knew it or not I'd had to jump in and pull out one or both of them more than once.

My attempt to explain to Alex, how Pa had insisted that we learn to swim was a bit awkward, but I continued with how now and again, they'd let us go down to the creek. There were more than a few sweltering days in August. My job was to watch the boys, not to swim. Course we wouldn't stay there but head for the Bay with the sandy beach. The boys were like a couple of bouncing dolphins and more than once one of those two would get in trouble and I'd have to go in and drag them out. I didn't tell him the part about how it wasn't easy in my long petticoat! Mum had said that was what I was to wear if I went in the water, and no one was to see me in that garb. I did add that Mum said girls don't swim.

At this Alex smiled and again reached out a finger to touch my arm.

He was intent on listening to me, so I continued telling him how Pa had taught me early on, which was good if I was to keep up with those twins.

"Once," I told him, "When I wasn't paying attention, those two floated out way too far. They had grabbed a piece of driftwood and it had carried them aways into the Bay. I couldn't swim that far and yelled at them to hang on and don't let go. All I could think was how'm I going to explain this when Mum finds out. That was when Mr. Bailey appeared. In his crabbing boat."

Alex smiled and seemed to be hanging on my every word. No one had ever given me this sort of attention.

"Mr. Bailey yelled at me that he had them and told me he'd bring them in."

I paused for a moment to wipe away a tear that appeared for no reason. But then continued. "He did. He picked up both and let them out in knee-high water. 'Course they didn't know whether to laugh or to cry. They'd been in a huge amount of danger."

Homesickness had taken over, but Alex had listened attentively and even nodded now and again His eyes seemed to be taking in all of me.

And then he was speaking, his blue eyes boring into me. "You need to be home. I want to help. I can't come with you but perhaps I could create a distraction and have you two slip overboard."

"But are you sure it's Rip and he's on this ship?"

Should I believe this? But then I was sure it had been his mourning dove whistle that I'd heard coming from the top of the mast.

"Yes," he answered. "I'm quite sure. He said he was from your island. We could somehow get you overboard. If luck is with us and the current, it wouldn't take more than a piece of board to keep you afloat."

Try as I might I couldn't help looking at him. He was a good deal taller than I was and as slender as a frond of marsh grass. And although we were surrounded by the fading light, I could see his eyes. They were as blue as the sky and seemed to have a deep caring. He was clean-shaven unlike many of the sailors. I think my heart skipped a beat. Why did I feel this way I wondered? I'd never had any interest in boys. At school, they were all younger and they all left anyway before turning 16. They were needed at home with farming, or their water-men dads needed them to help, so none stayed around.

My mind didn't want to make a decision as to what to do. But how could we stay here? What if I was found out? I didn't really want to leave this tall and confident midshipman. But he could help us and although we would be taking a huge chance, we may not get another.

"I would go with you," he said again, "but I'd be shot along with both of you if caught. It would be less of a risk if you went without me."

The dark had wrapped around us. We knew we were taking a chance chatting, but few were around, and most were busy cleaning up the mess from all the chaos in the Baltimore Harbor.

"I will help you if I can," he said. For a moment only his fingers reached out to touch my arm and then he turned abruptly and moved further down the deck.

LAND OF THE FREE. . .

The wind was calm, the sails slack, we were nearly still in the water. Off to the east, I was sure I could see our island, but the darkness was almost complete. For a fleeting moment, I wondered if this was to be the last view I'd have of home? In moments only we would be passing it by. The sky was dark. The sun had done its work for the day.

And then there he was. The world's worst pest!

I was so glad to see him. I tried to remain calm and nodded only. It wouldn't do to see two young American captives talking. I made myself busy, trying to look like one of the seamen as I rubbed the railing with a scrap of cloth, trying to get it to shine.

He was next to me. His voice was low. "If we lef' now, we could make it to shore." His dark arms continued in slow motion as he gave all his attention to sweeping the deck. His hat was pulled low, his eyes shaded.

I tried to give an acknowledging nod then bent to pick up a few of the splintered boards to add to the accumulating pile near the mast. Each piece would no doubt be used to make repairs. Something always needed attention, and nothing was ever wasted.

Rip continued sweeping. "We's headin' out of the Bay and down into the south." His voice was barely above a whisper.

The south? Where I wondered. Alex had said that too. The south was a very big area. What if they were headed to the Islands in the Caribbean or even South America? How would I ever make it back home?

I nodded to Rip hoping I wasn't being watched. Dark was all around us. We would need to do something soon if we were to survive. And I wondered if Cook would be searching me out to bring me back down to the galley.

Rip nodded towards a piece of scrap lumber that I had dragged over to the pile. If we could somehow get it back to the side and throw it overboard it could be a raft. It would have to be dark, or we'd be seen.

"Tonight," he said, and then answered with a "Yes Suh," as an officer approached telling him he was needed up by the wheel to clean the area. I returned to polishing the rail. This wasn't on my list of duties, but no one knew that, and I did appear to look like I knew what I was about.

The crew was busy finishing up and heading for their bunks after a long day. The sails had been slack a good while. We were making little progress. The winds had died. We were barely moving. The masts creaked as we slid ever so slowly further down the Bay. The waters were calm, nearly flat.

I heard the call of a mourning dove.

And there he was again, standing next to me, with broom in hand. "It be time," he said.

I must have looked doubtful or maybe even distrustful. We didn't have a real plan. And this was an 11-year-old boy whose favorite pastime was teasing anyone who crossed his path. He wasn't an adult or even close. Not only that, could he really swim?

"I wanna go home too," he said as if to reassure me. "I don' belong on no British brig." His voice was low, meant only for my ears. The deck was quiet with only one officer back with the helmsman.

The watchman was approaching us. Rip began his slow methodical sweeping looking for all the world as if this was his one and only job.

It was Alex the midshipman. I thought it best to stay concealed in the shadows. He moved closer to me and spoke in nearly a whisper. "If you're found missing, I'll say you were with Doc Beanes and the other two on the sloop heading to Baltimore. I doubt if anyone really knows where you're supposed to be. They won't turn around to try to find one galley slave and they may not even notice that your young friend is no longer on board." His voice was low.

I whispered, "we're ready."

Rip emerged from the shadows. He nodded that he too was ready.

"Come along then," said Alex. "We'll do this quickly as most of the crew are in their hammocks. There's only the helmsman and the officer back by the wheel."

He picked up the end of a couple of banged together boards. They were wide and seemed to be substantial, anyways enough for a makeshift raft. Together with Rip, he tossed them over the side. There was a sizeable splash.

"Quick now," he said as he grabbed my elbow. His eyes were boring into me. "Be careful," he whispered and gave me a quick hug. "A wonderful disguise." There was half a smile. "Now," he said, "over you go." He lifted me up. "We will meet again," he whispered. His eyes for a moment flashed merriment. "On Poplar Island."

And over I went like a done-with sack of potatoes.

I landed with a splash, disappearing under the waves. The water seemed icy as I kicked my way to the surface. There was another splash. It had to be Rip. It was so dark; I was sure I could hear him, but I couldn't see him.

"Go," he said. I could hear that clearly enough. I could hear the splash of him swimming.

How could the water be so cold I thought? It wasn't even autumn yet. I tried to kick and remember my swimming. I was trying to follow the splashing noise Rip was making. I was sure the floating boards, weren't that far off, and I could just see the splashing. My legs took over.

Rip yelled, "Over here." I could hear him and just barely see him in the darkness. "Over here," he kept saying. Now he was really yelling if you could yell while whispering. But if they saw us from the ship, who knew what they'd do to us.

And they did! I wasn't sure just what they yelled, but shots were fired. Fired at us! Why I wondered? Couldn't it have been a man overboard? Someone must have seen us.

Then that New England clipped accent was yelled from back by the wheel. "Let it go. What the devil are you jacktars shootin' at?"

The guns stopped. We could hear murmuring from on board, but the words floated off into the darkness.

I was sinking. My legs were tangled in my oversized pant legs. I couldn't kick. I was going to run out of breath. My arms weren't taking me forward. I gagged and sputtered on the water that wouldn't let me breathe. I was sure I was a goner. I just knew I was taking my last breath when a hand grabbed my arm. He was a lot stronger than I thought. He nearly yanked my arm out of the socket as he pulled me to the raft.

I grabbed one of the splintery planks. I was exhausted. I had nearly drowned. I coughed and spat out the brackish water that wanted to choke me. Rip banged me on the back. He was halfway on with one leg and one arm clinging to the tippy raft. I wasn't helping. My legs were heavy, my arms were turning numb. I was tired.

"C'mon," said Rip, "Yer gonna have to help me. Ye think I wanna be doin' this?"

But it wasn't going to work. The boards were too light weight to get up on. We were going to have to just hang on and see which way the current would take us. The other board was gone.

Worn out so soon, I wanted to put my head down and close my eyes. Maybe this wasn't the best decision. I watched the ship drift off in near silence, the winds were calm, their sails were slack. The darkness surrounded it, swallowing it up. It disappeared into the blackness of the night.

AND THIS BE OUR MOTTO –
"IN GOD IS OUR TRUST"…

The current wasn't strong. We were barely moving. We watched as the ship glided without a sound into the darkness of the night, taking them out of the Bay. They were done with Baltimore. South, I'd heard them say. But to where south? Far past our island no doubt.

The breezes weren't more than a whisper. With the winds at almost a dead calm, it was going to take some time for them to make any progress. The night air was barely moving. The seas were flat. And did I really care? I was done with them, and with luck by the light of day they would be far out of sight.

Try as I might I could see little. I was sure I'd seen my island earlier, but now in the blackness of night it had disappeared. Maryland's western shore had vanished too in the darkness and even if I could see it, it wouldn't have helped. I knew almost nothing about it. The two shores were like two separate countries. So far from each other, separated by this huge Bay. How could it even be the same state?

And now, how was I ever going to get home? We could already be well past our island but how could I be sure? My legs were dragging behind me 'cause I wasn't able to hoist myself up onto our makeshift raft. One leg and one arm hung over the splintery board. Rip was balancing on the other side. We dozed, but not for long.

The moon had started to rise. It appeared to be only a few days away from being full. Reflecting off the quiet up and down motion of the water, it created a trail of light. Somehow it was comforting to see what I imagined could be a bright glowing path that would lead us home.

Shimmering off the water, it showed us where we were and what was around us. Which was nothing! We were alone. Maybe smack in the middle of this great expanse of water.

There was no land that could be seen. I knew it was out there, somewhere. I had seen it earlier, maybe it had even been our island. But it was going to take some work if we wanted to get over to our side of the Bay.

And then Rip, rubbing the sleep from his eyes, broke through the silence. "C'mon," he said, "Let's get movin'." His voice somehow lacked his usual confidence, but there wasn't much else we could do. "Come on roun' to my side and we can start kickin'," he said. His voice had no strength or conviction, and I wasn't sure if I could make it all the way over to his side.

"I don't want to," I said.

He must have heard the doubt in my voice. I had never paid much attention to him, seeing him only as an unnecessary pest. But he spoke with such certainty, I had to listen.

"You can do dis," he said. "You got it in you. You just don' know it yet. You got the spirit, you gots the brains, you got the good sense. Now," he said, "You use what you got and git on over here."

My mind was truly getting fuzzy, but I heard his sassy voice. I wanted to object. I didn't agree with him but feeling more hopeless and helpless than I'd ever felt, I inched my way round. Both hands clung to the boards, in fear that if I let go, I'd be a goner. My nails felt like cats' claws clinging to the roughness. For a moment only, my grasp slipped. His hand was out there. He grabbed my shirt and pulled me over.

"Now here," he said, "listen to me. Grab da board and hang on."

I did. It was splintery but I didn't care.

We were silent, giving more attention to our sleepiness than to where we were heading. We were heading west. We were going in the wrong direction. The moon was behind us. It was rising in the east.

"Turn it around," he said. "We's headin' away from home. Kick," he said. "C'mon we can do 'dis."

And however we did it, we changed our direction. Weak and cold, we continued a sort of kicking motion that ever so slowly propelled us forward.

"We don' have to do it all at once." He seemed so sure of himself. "We go slow. We gonna get 'dere, you'll see."

My confidence was flagging, and I had to ask why he was so sure we'd get there?

"It's a long way," I said.

"Well," he answered, "You got somethin' better to suggest?" And then in a voice so low, I wasn't sure if I heard it correctly, he said, "Been in this sits-u-ation 'fore."

"Stuck in the middle of the Bay?" I asked. My voice couldn't have been more than a whisper but I'm sure he heard the disbelief or maybe doubt.

"Well, dat' too, once," he answered. "In the middle of the Bay. But more like a sits-u-ation that was near impossible."

I could see him push his hat back maybe so's he could see better? Then I had to wonder, how on earth did he still have that danged ratty hat after jumping off the side of a ship? But then I wasn't meant to have the answers to everything.

"What do you mean impossible?" I asked, wanting to finish the conversation, but maybe just so's I'd stay awake.

"I been in more'n one impossible sits-u-ation," he said. "Won't do no good in the re-tellin'."

And that was as much as he was going to say.

"Now," he said, and it was more like a command. "Kick. Not to git tired, but to keep us movin'. See that land over there?" He was pointing down the path of the shimmery glow of the moon that ended at a very small lump just barely visible in the night sky. "Might get there sometime tomorrow but kickin' jus' might keep us warm if we's kickin' away the time."

That made me smile. Well almost smile. I

wasn't really up to pretending I was having a good time. When he wasn't being a tease and a pest, he could be counted on to say something that would bring a laugh. Now it seemed that even in the worst situation he could find something to tease about or share something he found amusing. But I guess this wasn't going to be one of those times.

"Yer Pa," he added, "Ain't gonna be one bit happy wif me if I don' git you to home safe and sound."

My Pa? But then I remembered. Pa had said that Rip had more good sense than most men he knew. 'Course Pa was never around when he was being such an annoyance!

And I wondered would Pa even know what had happened to me? Here I was, somewhere in the middle of the Bay. By my calculations, there was a slim chance of ever seeing home again. I put my head down again, fighting a despair that was creeping over me.

The fish and the crabs were no doubt already planning on supping on my bones.

AND THE WAR'S DESOLATION...

And so we kicked. Rip was right. It kept us warm, well not really warm, but it kept us moving forward. Slowly. But it was also near exhausting. We weren't moving at any great rate. At the speed we appeared to be going, I suspected we weren't going to get to dry land anytime soon. But we were moving, and maybe in the right direction. We had what would probably be called a mission or even a goal, which clearly wasn't more than just to save ourselves. I was getting groggy.

He knew I was falling behind regardless of my efforts to propel us forward to stay afloat. He needed to come up with something encouraging or maybe cheerful. So, of course never at a lack for words, said: "C'mon, how 'bout I teach you how to whistle?"

I could barely answer but said, "Thought you said girls can't whistle."

"Well look at ye," he said, "Yer not lookin'

much like a girl."

"O.K. then," I said, I guess I sort of smiled. There was no enthusiasm in the answer.

"Pucker up then and blow."

I did as I was told but it just made him snicker.

"No, no, no. Easy like. Y'er not tryin' to blow up a storm. Just ease that breath out." There was a tiredness in his voice too, but he was trying.

I was truly sorry I wasn't enjoying this lesson, especially 'cause he'd never offered to teach me before. And truly I tried, but it wasn't coming, besides which it meant I had to raise my head and that was just too much trouble.

He tried again. "C'mon, give me one more. Pucker up and blow easy."

Well sure enough, and I really wish I cared, the faintest of whistles came out. I wanted to smile, but I put my head back down and closed my eyes. He too was silent.

The night went on. It seemed like forever. We had seen the moon rise and cross the sky. It had given just enough light to see land to our east. It was now preparing for its descent into the western horizon. The sky had started to lighten. The early rays were dim but there was the promise of a new day

My mind was wandering. I was hungry. I was tired. And I was near freezing. I kept kicking. Not with much strength.

I wondered if perhaps there'd be another day where we would get to start all over again, that would maybe include a few good things. I was sorely tired of things not working out but maybe that was the way it was supposed to be. But I wondered, was I not meant to ever succeed at anything? Was life nothing more than a bunch of struggles?

These weren't good thoughts, and they certainly weren't getting us any closer to home. I should be doing more to be getting us out of this. I was the oldest. Rip was still so young. Would we make it?

Early morning clouds and a bit of leftover fog muted the sun, but it was visible through the haze. What came to mind was how many times Mum had told me to wear my bonnet — and I didn't. She'd said I was as brown as an Indian. Well, was that so bad? Now I was probably going to be scorched red.

I really didn't care. The day was lightening up some, enough so's we could see a land mass ahead of us. It was either the eastern shore of

Maryland or one of the islands out in the Bay.

Whichever. It didn't matter, we just had to get there. I wasn't sure how much longer we could last. And we had to stay awake. I dozed off now and again but not for long. I knew the dangers of letting go of what had become our life raft. Rip would smack my hand every now and again, maybe just to be sure I was awake. He had stopped talking, which for someone who always had something to say wasn't good.

"Rip," I said, "Whyn't you tell me what all has happened to you and where you came from." My voice wasn't very strong. We were both losing strength.

"No story to tell," he said. He laid his head on his outstretched arms, careful not to upset his hat.

"There's more there than you want us to know," I said, "And we just may not make it to shore so there's no harm in telling it."

I laid my head back down on my arms. "And you well know I'm not one to go chatting about things that don't concern me."

His voice wasn't very strong, it wasn't much above a whisper. "Came from away," he said, with one finger pointing behind us. "'Cross from your island." His voice was tired with an I don't care what happens sound.

"Not my Island," I said, which I knew was unnecessary.

"Well, it be where you was born," he said. He sighed but continued. "Came from the mainland," he said. "Other side of the Bay." He was quiet for a time, and I wasn't sure if he'd continue. But then, "Was on a big cotton plantation down in No'th Carolina. I was young. Five years old maybe. Cain't be sure." His voice was low, "Got into some trouble."

He pulled his hat lower. It was hard to tell if he would continue.

I tried to find a comfortable place to lay my head. My legs had stopped kicking. We weren't going to get to the shore soon enough, I could tell. There was a quiet uneven snore. That was all I heard.

BY THE DAWN'S EARLY LIGHT ...

Maybe it was the seagulls. They were squawking above us as they searched for their morning meal. Their screeching brought me around. I tried to remember where I was.

I think I said, "Oh no," and put my head back down. This couldn't be I thought. Tears wanted to fall.

"C'mon girl. Git yo'self together. This ain't the time to quit." It was Rip and he was talking to me. How could he be so perky? I think I'd nodded off while he was telling me a story.

"Was tellin' you stuff," he said. "You up and went to sleep. Think you was snorin'."

"Now how could I have done that?" I asked. He knew it was my feeble attempt at humor. My voice wasn't much more than a whisper and I have no idea how I could have found humor in anything. "Well tell me your story," I said. I wasn't sure if he heard me.

His voice lacked strength too, but he went

on. "What I was tryin' to tell you was dey was gonna sell me at auction." There was a great sigh. "Do yeh know what that's like?" he asked. "No Ma, no Pa to come git you." He stopped. I know he didn't want to continue but whatever would keep us moving and awake would work, so he started up again.

"You still listenin'?" he asked. I nodded and wondered if he could see me. "If we both kick, maybe git us somewhere." I could hear his feet kicking; his eyes were focused on the land barely visible in the distance. The board was waterlogged and slippery. It wasn't very wide and not very thick, but it was long and was still floating.

He started again. "Well, some ol' grandma had tol' me to leave. She said I was strong enuf to walk a distance to get away. She say if they sells me, no tellin' where I'll end up." He gave a great sigh and much of what he was saying was muffled. "Don't know who see was, but she say stay out of sight. She say if I went far enuf north I could be free." He stopped.

And then closer to a mumble. "Last words I hear from her was tain't gonna be easy. She said there's gonna be one trouble after another. Don't much matter who you are – happens to everyone." He sighed and paused for a bit and then started again, "What matters is what ya gonna do about it and so far it be pretty good for me." His voice got stronger, "Got outa more than a few messes. I'm still here no matter what's beatin' me down."

Think that was what Pa had tried to tell me now and again. Had I even listened? And here I was listening to this kid who I was probably going to drown with!

I could feel the water moving as he kicked his legs, so I did too. It moved us forward. Slowly, but we were at least moving. There was no great speed, but bit by bit we were getting closer to the land. Maybe there was a chance we'd make it.

"Then?" I asked. My thought was to somehow stay awake and maybe not slip into the water which would be the end of it all. I was so cold. The water may have been warm but not to two soaked and bedraggled escaped sailors. Sailors I thought. Really? But what else could we have been?

He did go on. I was glad. "I left. Was caught once and dat's when my legs got beat. It was so's I'd stay put and wouldna' try to run off again." He gave a half-laugh. "Didn't stop me. They put shackles 'round my legs too. 'Course my legs was so skinny I slipped right outa' 'em."

There was a great sigh. "Then I run again," he said. "It took more'n a few days but made it to the shore. Heard them danged dogs," he said. He paused and I wasn't sure if he'd continue. I put my head down on my arms to rest. I really wanted to cry. Not only for our predicament but for all humanity – that I was part of this foolish world where things like this could happen.

My hair was wet and matted and hung over my eyes so's I really couldn't see him, just hear him. And he began again. I was glad.

"It was comin' on dark. Had no place else to go. There be a ship tied up. Haulin' cotton north. I tucked up in some of them bales of cotton that they was puttin' on board."

There was a great sigh and I wasn't sure if he'd continue but then, "Them dogs lost interest, anyways I didn't hear 'em no more. Then they found me, maybe a couple o' days out. Hidin' in that cotton." His voice had gotten weaker. He truly sounded as about tired as one can get, but he kept on, maybe knowing we were both going to slip under the water if we didn't do something.

"Thought dey was gonna string me up. Jumped overboard. I knew somethin' 'bout swimmin'. Not enuf to git me outa the sits-u-ashun I was in but hung onto a piece of drift-wood. I maybe floated for a couple a days. Not sure. Then one mornin' - dat's when dat water-man pull me outa da water." He sighed, "I was about dead!"

He rubbed at his eyes. "And" he added, "here I am, right back where's it all began." I thought I could hear an almost half chuckle. "Wonder if this is how I's s'posed to spend my life? Floatin' around in this Bay. Nowhere to settle?"

"Stay with us," I said. Did I really just say that? But then added, "My pa would love it." I think he laughed. Well snickered anyhow. "He thinks you're really smart."

Hardly believing I'd just said that I added, "If you've already done this, you'll know how to get us out of this sits-u-ashun that we now find ourselves in." I wasn't laughing at him, just happened to enjoy how he could say sits-u-ashun, managing to give it the importance it needed. I could tell he was smiling, so no harm done.

"Dis what we gonna do," he said. We keep lookin' fo'ward. Get our sights on one thing. We face that piece of land stickin' up. See it over there? We kicks our legs 'til we get to land." He paused a moment. He was waiting for an answer, but none was forthcoming. "You got some better idea?" he asked. His voice wasn't much above a whisper.

"Well," I said, "guess that's about all we can do. And" I added, and I really didn't want to talk anymore, "Looks like we might be having a good day." I almost wanted to laugh. Why would I care about a good day if I was about to slip under the waves and never be seen again? But I pushed the hair out of my eyes and squinted into the distance. "Can't see any clouds and it appears we're not that far out." I put my head back down to rest.

"Currents changing," he said. "Seems to be pushin' us towards whatever shore that is."

"I need to get home." I didn't really need to say that. I kicked my feet the way Pa taught me. It moved us forward. Not with any great speed, but the current was with us, and we were moving a bit. I think the kicking warmed me up some.

"I think I like our island," I said. Not sure if he heard me, guess I really didn't care. I know my voice was getting faint. And to think, my fondest wish was to get away from this lonely and desolate island

But then, "It's where I need to be." I was sure of it. But why does everything have to fall apart before some things become clear?

My legs began to paddle again, in rhythm to Rip's kicking. Tired, hungrier than I'd ever been and wanting to rest, but wanting to stay awake. With each kick, I was sure we were getting closer to shore.

That was when Rip said, "Look!" I was too tired to look or even lift my head. "No," he said, "ya gotta look."

I did. And there on the horizon was a small sloop with its sails full out. I was squinting in the morning light as I tried to get the hair and water out of my eyes. And then I had to smile. It was the boat with the two unmatched sails. One darker than the other. The darker one with more than a few patches. The blue patch near the top of the mainsail covering the largest tear. Didn't matter. The sails worked in harmony.

Matthew had said it was the only way the sail could be saved, put a patch on the torn spot.

Rip pulled off his hat. His arm seemed stiff and not wanting to work right, but he held that hat high and waved it at Matthew.

He was sitting on the other side, hidden by the sail. He couldn't see us. Rip yelled a loud

"Heeeeey!" Nothing.

Matthew stayed on course. He was intent on reaching the shore. And then, an unexpected gust of wind forced him to come about. He easily moved to the other side of the boat. And then - He saw us!

We stopped kicking and just hung on as he changed course. The sails had been luffing and a bit slack but now both were filled with the wind. He stood tall, with one hand on the tiller, guiding the boat.

He waved to us.

He had seen us.

The sails pushed the boat forward with the freshening breeze. It danced across the waves as it picked up speed, skimming across the water. It was bearing down on us.

The sun broke through the clouds, casting a golden glow all around. The small sloop with Matthew at the helm was fairly dancing over the waves, racing towards us. This was going to be a good day.

Blest with vict'ry and peace . . .

THE END

~ FACTOIDS ~

- In December, 1814, The Treaty of Ghent was signed ending the War of 1812. However, a battle still raged in New Orleans. News of the treaty did not reach there until after that battle had ended January, 1815.

- There were more than 10,000 U.S. impressed seamen in the British Navy in 1812. The practice ceased at the war's end in 1814. The War of 1812 was often referred to as the Battle of Impressment.

- 15,000 American lives and 8,600 British lives were lost during the War of 1812. The number of native Americans who also lost their lives is not known.

- Francis Scott Key wrote much of the poem *The Defence of Ft. M'Henry*, while detained in the Port of Baltimore in 1814. It was later put to the music of an English drinking song and given the title *The Star-Spangled Banner*. In 1931 it became America's national anthem by congressional resolution.

- Doctor William Beanes, an American, did in fact patch up many of the British soldiers who had been wounded. British soldiers testified in writing that he had aided them. Through the efforts of Francis Scott Key, a lawyer, and Col. John Skinner, a U.S. Government agent, he was given his freedom.

- Mary Pickersgill was contracted to sew the gigantic 30' x 42' flag that flew at Ft. McHenry. It had 15 stars and 15 stripes, which recognized the two states that had most recently been admitted to the Union: Vermont and Kentucky.

- During the Battle at Ft. McHenry four Americans lost their lives. Of those casualties, one was a civilian woman who was carrying supplies to the troops.

- Poplar Island was raided by Indians in 1637 eradicating all the residents. In 1777 the island was raided by the British, who burned every house and seized all the livestock. The island of less than 100 residents was abandoned in the 1920s because of erosion.

- The U.S. Army Corps of Engineers is restoring Poplar Island using dredged material from the Baltimore Harbor area. It is now designated as a wildlife refuge and can be visited by boat. Information can be found at: www.poplarislandrestoration.com

Mulberry Cove

Amelia had been safely tucked away at a quiet and comfortable boarding school in England. It had been her home for years. A war was raging in America. A war she knew nothing about. Her Uncle had sent for her. She was to come to his plantation at once. It was in a remote area of the south, in the heart of slave country. They raised cotton she was told.

Amelia risks a dangerous journey across the ocean to a strange and hostile country to meet with the Uncle. But he's nowhere to be found!

Why had they sent for her? Why was the uncle nowhere to be found?? And was this really her aunt? How could she get back to her school, the only home she'd ever known?

The Civil War was raging as Amelia struggles with the demands and upheavals and unending responsibilities of her new home. A home that she didn't want and one that she wasn't sure she would survive.

Antietam
Waking the Fury

Emily at 15 is bored and annoyed with just about everything and everybody. Tired of her chores and irritated by the endless care of three younger sisters, she would like to have a life of her own. Her parents are absent; her Father is off fighting a war she doesn't understand and her Mother has left for Pennsylvania. As the eldest of the four sisters, she must take responsibility for her home and family. When the bloodiest battle of the Civil War is fought almost on her doorstep she is unwillingly pressed into service. Emily is called on to make decisions and to take charge of wounded soldiers while fending off the invading troops and protecting her younger sisters. Life changes forever as she discovers a courage that she did not know she possessed. Strengths emerge as she stands up for her beliefs while sheltering the enemy and caring for a runaway slave, both of which hold very serious consequences. In this remarkably accurate depiction of the Battle of Antietam, a legend is once more uncovered. It involves a mass of very angry bees. This dangerous, stinging swarm may well have had an influence on the outcome of that fateful day in 1862.

Jennie Wade
A Girl From Gettysburg

It had been foolish to stay but now there was no choice. It was anyone's guess what the outcome would be. Nothing was as it should be. Oddly, the Confederate troops were pouring in from the north and Union troops were marching in from the south. They arrived in droves. The town was not prepared for what happened during the early days of the summer, 1863. Jennie, a young local girl, did her best to keep up with the demand for bread and water and medical care for the troops. Her brothers were scattered, her sister would soon be having a baby, her mother was not bearing up well and Jack, her intended, had not been heard from in weeks. It was a time and place that would be recorded in American history forever. A time marked by the largest number of casualties in the Civil War. It was Gettysburg, Pennsylvania, a small, unremarkable town; an easily forgotten town that would live in infamy and one that history would never forget. Of the almost 50,000 casualties of that encounter in early July, only one civilian was killed. This is her story. The story of Jennie Wade, a dedicated young woman thrown into the middle of one of Americans' most tragic times.

Mists of the Blue Ridge

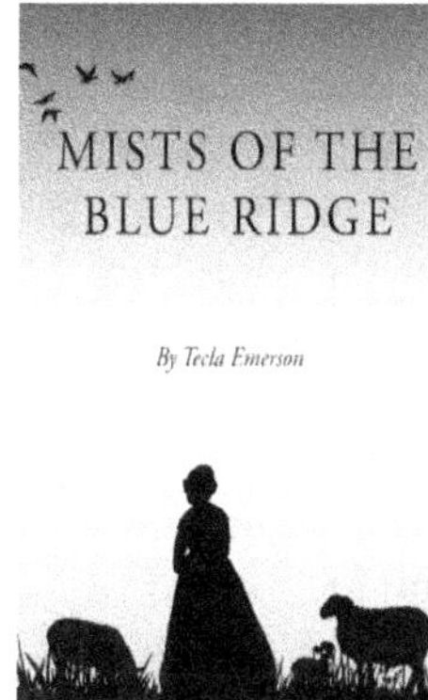

Olivia lived a quiet and protected life tucked away on a farm in the Blue Ridge Mountains. It was far from the great war that had been raging between the North and the South. She had little interest in the who and the why of it all, and wasn't even sure where her sympathies lay. Then, without warning, the conflict surrounded her. At 16, she was ill prepared for the responsibilities that were thrust on her.

This is her story. It's a tale that tells of courage, determination and survival during one of America's most trying times.

Hidden in the Early Light

a tale of the Irish famine

Katy was 16 when the hard times came. Her father disappeared in the night and her mother left her with a tiny baby sister. She was suddenly thrust into the role of caretaker. It was a responsibility she didn't want. The farming life was not for her and now she had to find a way to survive and to keep her younger brothers from starving. How could she ever be free of a life she hadn't chosen?

It was the 1840s and thousands were dying from the great potato famine, one of history's most dreadful events.

This is Katy's story, the story of how a young girl survived by using her wits, determination and courage.

Shadows in the Fog

A Block Island Tale

Milly lived on an island far away from the mainland. She was an orphan and there was no one to care for her. Sent to live in a house filled with boys she was pressed into the role of cook and caretaker. Her life became that of a servant.

When an unfortunate incident took place that threatened to scar her forever, she was sent to live with an angered and bitter veteran of the Civil War.

Living the life of a recluse and with battle scars of his own, he keeps his past hidden from all. Hidden until Milly comes to stay.

This is the tale of a young girl's quest for survival and how she brings herself out of the depths of despair as she learns of her mysterious past. Uplifting and compelling, the tale follows Milly as she matures and accepts all that life has given her.

Gift of the Winds
A Tale of Hendricks Head Lighthouse

In the late 1800s a ferocious nor'easter traveled up the New England coast. It forced a three-masted schooner up on the rocks. It was within sight of the Hendricks Head Lighthouse. History says there were no survivors. However, a trunk was found that had been washed ashore. It held a most unusual and interesting surprise.

The tale unfolds through Abigail's diary. It tells of the unfortunate event that condemned her to the life of a recluse in Ireland. Life is difficult for her, but determined to survive; an inner strength takes over. Alone, she sets out for a new life in America.

Andersonville:

The Long Journey Home

Hock snuck off in the dark of night to join the Union Army. He was too young to be part of the fighting force but now, taller than most, he easily joined their ranks.

Wounded in the battle at Petersburg he was captured and sent to a Confederate prisoner-of-war camp – a camp so horrid, it is still written of today. As one more of Andersonville's nameless inmates, he was given a number. Identified as "Unknown 9586," he was thrown on the death cart and hauled out as one of the dead. "Unknown 9586," did not rest in peace. Leaving the site of his burial, he set out for the north. Alone, starving, wounded and unarmed he began his journey. This is his story. From the hills of Vermont to the sights and scenes of horror that are found on battlefields and then to his final destination. It's the tale of prisoner #9586 – Unknown. The prisoner who missed his own burial.

Indentured Servant

"My being for ever banished from your sight?" Who was this "...undutiful and Disobedient Child" who in 1756 penned a letter to her father in England? What had she done to so offend him? Why, as a well educated young girl, had she become an indentured servant? Why was she alone? In her letter, she pleads with her father to forgive her and to at least send her a bit of clothing. "...almost naked, no shoes nor stockings to wear."

Here, within these pages, the mystery of Elizabeth Sprigs is revealed. It is a tale based on a single letter sent from Baltimore so long ago.

The Oregon Trail:

Pathway to the West

Maddie knew the trip wouldn't be easy. Her mother and older brother were no longer with them and Hannah, her little sister, was hers alone to care for. And Hannah was mute. Mute for reasons no one knew.

It would take months to arrive at their destination. Months that would include accidents, floods, Indian attacks and disease. The losses along the trail were both huge and unexpected. Would they ever reach the West, the land of their new home?

They traveled in covered wagons, on horseback and many times on foot. They risked all that they had, over the rough and not well-organized trails. It was a time filled with mystery and unknowns. There were few firsthand accounts of what lay before them and for some of the travelers the long trip would have disastrous results.

It was 1845. A small group of daring and brave pioneers set out with high hopes and all their worldly goods to head for a new life. A new life in what was soon to become the Oregon Territory.

www.ingramcontent.com/pod-product-compliance
Lightning Source LLC
Chambersburg PA
CBHW070355200726
48294CB00003B/929